NAIROBI HEAT

MUKOMA WA NGUGI

MELVILLEHOUSE
BROOKLYN, NEW YORK

MELVILLE
INTERNATIONAL
CRIME

To Meja Mwangi and David Mailu for blurring the margins

Acknowledgements

Without much discussion and constant critique a novel such as this would be all the poorer. So, thanks to Kristin Waller, Keenan Schofield, Megan Frantz and my wife Maureen Burke for their candid, useful and some might say merciless responses. Also thanks to Sophie Hoult at David Godwin Associates and Penguin South Africa for investing time, energy and resources in the project. And, finally, thanks to James Woodhouse for making the editing process not only painless but more importantly creative.

Nairobi Heat
© 2010 Mukoma Wa Ngugi

First Melville House printing: August 2011

Melville House Publishing
145 Plymouth Street
Brooklyn, NY 11201
www.mhpbooks.com

ISBN: 978-1-935554-64-6

Printed in the United States of America

1 2 3 4 5 6 7 8 9 10

Library of Congress Cataloging-in-Publication Data

Mukoma wa Ngugi.
  Nairobi heat / Mukoma Wa Ngugi.
     p. cm.
  ISBN 978-1-935554-64-6
  1. Nairobi (Kenya)--Fiction. 2. African American detectives--Fiction.
3. Murder victims--Fiction. I. Title.
PR9381.9.M778N3 2011
823'.92--dc23
                                                    2011026215

A BEAUTIFUL BLONDE IS DEAD

❝A beautiful young blonde was dead, and the suspect, my suspect, was an African male. I was travelling to Africa in search of his past. What I found there would either condemn or save him. As you can imagine my business was urgent.

How many times had I thought of Africa? Not many, I'm afraid. Yes, I knew of Africa. After all it was the land of my ancestors; a place I vaguely longed for without really wanting to belong to it. I might as well say it here: coming from the US there was a part of me that had come to believe it was a land of wars, hunger, disease and dirt even as my black skin pulled me towards it. So how many times had I thought of Africa? Not many, not in a real way.

The funny thing though was now that I was actually in a plane on my way to Africa I found myself surrounded by whiteness – the passengers, the crew and the pilots. It was early May, and I gathered from the conversations around me that my fellow passengers were business people, tourists and hunters from Texas. The usual, I supposed.

I looked outside, watching the full moon hover in the sky

beyond the tip of the aeroplane wing, childishly imagining it to be catching a free ride. We travelled for a while like that, the moon surfing on the wing, until the pilot warned us, in that proper British accent that we have come to associate with efficiency, to prepare for landing.

The moon leapt back into the sky as we pierced the clouds and below I saw what looked like an island of lights engulfed by perfect darkness. Then we landed and everyone clapped. I was tired and a little tipsy from the complimentary Budweisers the crew had offered me, and so it was that, a little bit drunk, I took my first steps in Africa.

❝ At customs I flashed my passport and my badge. The clerk didn't even give my gun permit a second look, just shook his head and said, 'You Americans, you really love your guns, eh?' as he waved me through.

I didn't have any luggage other than what I had carried off the plane and so soon enough I found myself outside the airport in what felt like a market – a wall of people shouting and heckling, selling newspapers, phone cards, even boiled eggs. Blackness suddenly surrounded me, and coming from plane full of whites I felt relief and panic at the same time – it was as if I was in camouflage, but it was very poor camouflage because at six foot three and two hundred and twenty pounds I towered over everybody. People here were short and spare, and I felt full of useless excess – as if I had extra body parts. But it wasn't the people that stopped me in my tracks, it was the heat. The heat made New Orleans on a hot summer day feel like spring. Humid, thick and salty to taste, that was

Nairobi heat.

A taxi driver dressed in dirty white slacks made a grab at my hand luggage. '*Mzungu*, *mzungu*, good rate for tourist,' he yelled, but I held on to my case.

I didn't know much Kiswahili but I knew from the guide book I had started reading on the plane that he was calling me a white man. It was a strange irony that I, an African American, a black American, was being called a white man in Africa, but I didn't make much of it, I just laughed and gently pushed him away. I should have told him I wasn't here to see lions and giraffes, I concluded as I waded through the crowd warding off all sorts of attempts to get me into this or that cab until I heard a deep voice calling me: 'Ishmael!'

Turning to find the voice I came face to face with one of the blackest men I had ever seen. I mean, I'm black but this brother was so black he looked blue. Standing around six foot, he was, like everyone else, on the spare side, but unlike everyone else he was, despite the heat, dressed smartly in a heavy brown leather jacket, black corduroys and tough looking leather safari boots.

'Ishmael, I presume,' my Kenyan counterpart from the Criminal Investigation Department said, bowing slightly before breaking into laughter. 'Stanley to Livingstone ... The explorers ... They say they discovered us, you know.'

'Yes,' I said, beginning to see the humour – one black American and one African playing explorer.

'My name is David, David Odhiambo,' he continued, reaching out to shake my hand. 'My friends and enemies call me O.'

As I shook O's hand I realised that I could not sense

him. Usually people trigger something in me – some sort of emotion: fear, attraction, warmth – but not O. He was just vaguely familiar. In fact, the only thing my senses did tell me was that underneath what was unmistakably Brut cologne there was a sharp undercurrent of marijuana, which explained his red eyes.

'Come, let's get out of this madness … Are you parked?' he asked as he reached for my rucksack.

I looked at him, puzzled.

He opened up his jacket to reveal one of those old .45s – something made long before either of us had been born.

'If you mean packing, then yes, I am,' I said, pulling my jacket open slightly so that he could see my Glock 17 – light, easy to use but deadly nonetheless.

'Good, otherwise I would have had to find you one of these bad babies,' he said and laughed again. I couldn't tell whether he was trying to sound American or not.

'Is there some place around here that we can go for a beer and talk?' I asked.

'Now you're talking my language, I know just the place for you,' O said as we made our way out to the parking lot and got into a beaten-up Land Rover.

❝ We drove for a while without talking. I was tired and excited at the same time, but out of the million little curiosities that clouded my mind I could think of nothing to ask, so I listened to O as he hummed a Kenny Rogers song – 'The Gambler' – which he interrupted every now and then with curses as we dipped in and out of the potholes that littered the road.

Soon up ahead I could see the city. 'Nairobi?' I asked, just to make conversation.

'Nairobbery,' O answered with a laugh. 'That is what we call it … but no worries, as long as we are in this,' he patted the dashboard, 'criminals will know not to mess with us.'

For a while I could still see the large island of city lights in front of me. Then, suddenly, O veered off the main road and onto a dirt track and the city disappeared from view. We travelled on, headlights tunnelling through the darkness, the beams glancing off long dry grass, short thicket bushes and wild sisal plants. We drove past a pineapple plantation and then turned into a short, dirty street that ran between two rows of poorly built wooden houses. Finally, just past a shaky wooden billboard with the words *You are now leaving Pineapple town* splashed across it we almost ran into a dilapidated bar that proclaimed itself to be *The Hilton Hotel*.

'Tomorrow, I will take you to the real Hilton,' O said as we climbed out of the Land Rover and made our way towards the wooden structure, 'but here you get a taste of the real Africa.'

Inside, the bar was lit by kerosene lamps that gave it a smell that was a cross between gasoline and burning cloth. In the dull light they provided I could see that the walls were covered with fading magazine posters for all sorts of things – Marlboro, Camel Lights, Exxon, McDonald's. The lamps also illuminated the patrons, and I quickly realised that The Hilton was full of the living dead – some men passed out on the counter, others so drunk that they were muttering to themselves without making a sound.

O and I found a table that didn't have a drunk on it,

and the bartender – a young woman dressed in a rainbow-coloured wrap – came to take our order.

'Are you hungry?' O asked.

I nodded and watched as O ordered some beer and two kilos of roast meat. There are two things that Kenyan men treasure beyond life itself, I was to learn: their Tusker beer and roast meat, *nyama choma*. Tusker *moto* – hot Tusker – and *nyama choma* is the fastest way to get information, say thank you, make and close a deal, express friendship or make peace.

'Ishmael, welcome to Africa,' O said as soon as our beers arrived. He raised his Tusker for a toast, sipped and leaned back in his chair. 'So, tell me, what can I do you for?'

I told him my story.

❝ A young blonde woman found murdered on the doorstep of a black man – an African. Of course it was going to be the story of the year.

If I was to give advice to black criminals, I would tell them this: do not commit crimes against white people because the state will not rest until you are caught. I mean, if a crime is not solved within the first forty-eight hours it has all but officially gone cold. But a black-on-white crime does not go cold. A beautiful blonde girl is dead and a week later I'm chasing after ghosts in Africa. Had it been a black victim I certainly wouldn't have been racking up overtime in Nairobi.

The call came at two in the morning. I jumped out of bed, surprised only by the address – 2010 Spaight Avenue, Maple Bluff – and five minutes later, dressed in black pants, a white dress shirt and a smart black jacket, I was on the road. I combed my hair on my way there – siren blaring, doing ninety miles an hour. You don't show up in Maple Bluff looking as if you have just woken up.

By the time I got to the scene the paramedics and cops from the Maple Bluff Police Department had already arrived. The residents of this little tax haven even had their own police and fire departments. No detectives though, and that's why I'd been called in, most probably on loan. My department makes thousands – and, if lucky, I get paid overtime.

The uniforms were just standing around, watching as the paramedics – who had just given up trying to revive the girl – returned their equipment to the ambulance. Neighbours, extremely white and dressed in those expensive shiny pyjamas, were looking on too. I asked them to go back into their homes – we would be knocking on their doors soon enough.

The girl was lying on the stairs; her long blonde hair strewn around her, the bright porch light beaming down as if she was on a theatre stage. She looked to be somewhere between eighteen and twenty. Her white shirt had been ripped open – by the paramedics, I later learned – exposing a full, braless chest. She was wearing a short pleated skirt, like a cheerleader's, knee-length white socks and white tennis shoes.

The first thought that came to mind was how beautiful she was – the red polish on her nails was flawless; her hair, though messy from the paramedics trying to shock her back to life, was still a glittery blonde; her eyes were closed and her face calm. She didn't even look lifeless, and I expected her to get up at any moment for the final curtain call.

Stepping back, I asked the uniforms where the owner of

the house was and they pointed inside. I would have expected him or her to be tripping all over the place, trying to help, or be hovering at the door, beside themselves with worry, but whoever owned the house obviously felt differently.

Walking around the girl, I stepped up onto the porch from the side. *Home Is Where The Heart Is* I read as I wiped my shoes on the mat and knocked on the door. There was no answer, but the door wasn't locked and so I let myself in.

Inside, the hallway was lit only by the flashing lights of the ambulances and police cars standing outside. All my instincts told me to draw my gun, so I did, steadying my flashlight in my left hand as I walked down a long passageway and into the sitting room.

'I tell them girl is dead,' a deep voice said in the dark.

I whirled around, pointing the flashlight in the direction of the voice.

'Why they mistreat her body?'

There was a man sitting in a leather lovers' seat, absently twirling an empty wine glass by its stem, and as I watched he reached over and turned on a table lamp by his side. In the sudden brightness I saw that he was immaculately dressed – a black-and-white pinstriped suit and a thin red tie, expensive brown patent leather shoes without socks.

'You found her?' I asked him, but it was more of a statement.

'Yes, I find her like that. I was out with friends for cocktails … Sammy's Lounge.'

As I put my gun away the man stood up – he was black, very tall, much taller than me, and so thin that his head seemed to be growing from his shoulders. He stretched out a bony hand that seemed to grow from the suit and grasped mine firmly.

'Their names?'

He gave me four names – I could look them up at the university, he said. They would vouch for him. He was very composed, no bulging carotid, shifty eyes or sweaty palms. None of the telltales that we are trained to look for.

'And what time did you leave Sammy's Lounge?'

'About twelve thirty. I walk. I like walk ... to wash whiskey out of my blood. Half an hour. Maybe more, maybe less, I get here. I call nine one one when I find her.'

'Did you use your cellphone?'

He handed it over to me. He had called the police at one thirty-three am. I pointed it out to him but he just shrugged.

'Your accent ... Where are you from?' I asked.

'My friend, everyone has accent ... mine just mean I speak two languages, French and Kinyarwanda. I am from Rwanda ... and Kenya. My name is Joshua Hakizimana. And yours, Detective?'

'You can call me Ishmael ... born and bred here in Madison, Wisconsin,' I replied, feeling very much like the village idiot in the face of his class and poise.

'Very, very sorry to hear that,' he said with a short laugh and pointed to a chair for me to sit. 'I teach at university. I am teacher of Genocide and also Testimony. You know what happen in ... ?'

'Was she one of your students?' I interrupted. I didn't need a history lesson

'No, never seen her. Not type that take my class.' He sounded dismissive.

'What type is that?'

'Bohemians and Peace Corps types… What you Americans call trust fund babies, no?' He broke into a short laugh.

Except for his unsettling calmness there was nothing to arouse suspicion. Whatever clues there were would be with the girl. Only an autopsy would tell us about her last hours. After that we would have to interview the neighbours, trawl the local bars for someone who might remember her, go through the last six or so years of university enrolments and missing persons files and hope we got a lucky break.

I asked Joshua if I could look around and he agreed. I left him and wandered off by myself, switching on the lights as I went. The place was huge but it was the bedroom that interested me. Perhaps this whole mess was just a lover's quarrel gone too far – sometimes things are that simple. She was a student of his and wanted to break it off. Or he wanted to break it off and she had threatened to expose him to the university authorities.

I finally found it. There was only a huge bed, immaculately made up, and a nightstand with nothing on it except a lamp. I opened the closet and found rows and rows of suits, each ready with a black shirt and matching shoes beneath it. In the adjoining bathroom there was a single toothbrush on the sink next to a tube of organic toothpaste. The medicine cabinet was empty. It didn't look like I was going to find anything useful, so I went back downstairs to find him sitting in the same position, with his wine glass now half full.

I pointed to his shoes and asked about the socks.

'Sometimes I forget myself. Absent-minded professor,

no?' he said with mock sadness as he stood up to walk me to the door.

'How did you know the girl was dead?' I asked as I gave him my card.

'Detective, where I come from death is a companion, like lover or good friend. Always there,' he said as I stepped outside.

'We found this over there,' one of the MBPD cops said to me, pointing to the fence as I made my way off the porch. It was a needle, half full of what I knew to be heroin.

I looked closely at the girl's arms and easily found the single needle mark, slightly bloody. On the face of it, it looked like an overdose or a suicide but not a murder. This was Maple Bluff after all – a cat up the tree, stolen stop signs, an occasional drunk and unruly grandmother visiting from up-country perhaps, but not murder.

There was nothing more for me to do that night, so I went home to write up my report. Thank God for technology – I could do it all online with a cold beer and slice of pizza. Back in the day, I would've been up to my neck in paperwork.

But as I was typing little details began to bother me. The walls of the house, for example, had been empty – no paintings, no photographs. It had been like being in one huge hotel room, impersonal yet inhabited. How could he live in that house without leaving a trace of himself? But that wasn't a crime, I told myself. And perhaps the house wasn't home for him; perhaps somewhere in Africa was a house full of photos of a smiling wife, kids and a little dog called Simba that only ate crocodile meat. But even if that was the case, how could a college professor afford a home in Maple Bluff? The taxes themselves were enough to feed and clothe a family of six. Something didn't add up – a beautiful blonde girl dead on the doorstep of an African professor. A suicide or an accidental overdose on a stranger's front porch? No, it was too random to be random. And I've seen some fucked up shit. Like this guy who killed a man as he fetched his morning *Wisconsin State Journal* and left a note on him: *A STRANGER KILLS A STRANGER. ONCE. YOU WILL NEVER CATCH ME. SIGNED, RANDOM*. With today's forensics as long as the victim has even the slightest connection to the killer, sooner or later we get the fucker. But the Random Killer case was different – the victim and the killer were strangers connected only by a theory we barely understood.

To cut a long story short, the killer made one fatal mistake – he had left a partial thumbprint on the note. Five years later there was a fire in a hotel basement that was put out without much damage, but because we suspected arson we fingerprinted all the hotel guests and employees and cross-checked the fingerprints against our database. We didn't catch the arsonist but it turned out that our Random Killer had been holed up in the hotel doing all sorts of things with a hooker. Nothing much to him in the end; just a local pharmacist with a loving wife and kids.

When he was brought in I looked him straight in the eye and told him that he had fucked up. A perfect crime has no motive. And if there is no motive, then there's no crime? But he just looked up at me with pity in his eyes. 'You are a fool,' he said. 'Did it not occur to you, Detective, that I was trying to prove that chance is not random?'

I don't know what the hell he meant by that, and he

refused to say another word – to me, to his lawyers, to his kids and wife – but this much I did know: there had to be a connection between the white girl and the African professor. If I found it, I would be closer to understanding what had happened. There had to be a connection, but what was it?

I was tired as hell but I woke up early that morning to go see the coroner – one strange dude.

'Always stuck with the real pretty ones, ain't we, Ishmael?' Bill Quella – BQ for short – said as he pulled the girl out of storage, his Southern twang, sing-songy and a little high-pitched for a man, echoing off the tiles.

'Unlucky in life, lucky in death I guess,' I answered.

BQ laughed a nervous squeal of a laugh. He, like everybody else I worked with, knew my wife had left me. What they didn't know was that she had left me because I was a black cop. At least that is what she'd said. I didn't understand. How could I be a traitor to my race when I was protecting it? But then there were lots of things I didn't understand around that time, like how you could ask a man to choose between his life's work and love?

'Do you want to know what she chowed down before she met her untimely death?' BQ asked, pulling back the sheet to reveal the girl.

The glow she had had in death was gone. With cross-stitched sutures running along her chest, across her belly and below her hairline – where BQ had cracked her open – she looked like a white leather mannequin. By the time BQ had finished with them the dead always looked like the dead.

'Spare me the details … ' I grumbled, 'just get to it.'

'Well, Detective Ishmael, you sure gonna love this. It was

murder made to look like an overdose.'

BQ paused for dramatic effect, but I wasn't biting. 'How do you know?' I asked, careful to keep the surprise out of my voice.

'Real easy ... For a start the heroin was injected into her arm after she was long gone. Exhibit A: no trace of it in her blood. And B: see this ... ' He pointed to her arm. 'This is the only needle mark on her whole precious body. She was no addict.'

More questions than answers. 'How did she die then?'

'She was asphyxiated. A pillow over her head I would guess ... ' he said. 'She died from oxygen deprivation. Poor thing was murdered.'

'What time?'

'My guess? Somewhere between eleven pm and one am.' BQ paused. 'Look here, Detective, I might be going off half-cocked, but whoever killed her didn't want to destroy her. My guess is it was someone who knew her well, someone who might even have loved her ... '

❝ I made it to the Madison Police Station around nine am to find it in chaos. Someone had called the press – someone always calls the press – and they had set up camp on the steps, pulling in dozens of civilians, all of them struggling to see what was going on. We should have been better prepared. We should have had some kind of media strategy. But instead, as I pushed through the crowd, I saw the Police Chief, Jackson Jordan, standing in the eye of the storm, trying to calm everyone down. He would hold a press conference with the

Mayor as soon as they had more information, he was telling the assembled throng as calmly as he could.

Luckily the press didn't know I was the lead detective and I made it to the Chief's office relatively unscathed. He came in shortly, huffing and puffing, calling the press all sorts of names. I knew what the problem was. Jackson Jordan was the black police chief of a mostly white police force in a mostly white town. The victim was a young white woman and the main suspect, even though not officially, was a black man, an African. There would be the facts of the case and the politics of the case, and the two never mix well. None of this was said between us, we just understood it.

Jackson Jordan had been elected because he was tough on crime. That is, he was tough on black crime. I respected the Chief well enough to work under him, but it wasn't always easy. He was liable to pander to politics, and I always followed the evidence to wherever it led – to the cat selling two rocks by the corner liquor store; to the Mayor or the Governor himself. But like I said, I liked him well enough to work under him, and at the end of the day we all had a grudging respect for him.

'Chief, I'm working this case alone,' I said.

My partner, a white guy, had just retired and I knew where this was going – a white partner for the nigger cop to make everyone feel safe. But I wasn't going to have it. If I was going to get a partner, I wanted one for the right reasons, not to balance the racial math.

'Who's the girl?' the Chief asked, ignoring my statement.

As I didn't know I gave him BQ's report instead. He sank into his chair and ran his hand over his balding head. Now in his fifties, the Chief was the kind of fat that cops get when they spend too much time behind the desk – not an obese fat, just a lazy roundness that seems unbecoming for a police officer.

'Tell me about the African … ' the Chief said.

There was nothing much to tell beyond the bare facts. Joshua had told me that he had found her on his doorstep, dead. He had an alibi and his place was clean; no signs of a struggle inside or outside. There had been no visible scratches or marks on him. And he hadn't given himself away with any of the usual telltales. The body seemed to have literally fallen on his doorstep.

'Did you tear the place apart?' the Chief asked.

I hadn't. My first instinct was that whatever had happened hadn't happened in Joshua's house – I had been convinced of it and BQ's estimated time of death had pretty much confirmed my suspicions. I tried to explain but the Chief said he would send forensics in anyway. 'A fucking murder,' he muttered under his breath. 'Just what I need … ' He paused. 'Listen, this African of yours is some sort of hero back in his country.'

He handed me a folder from his desk. It contained newspaper and magazine articles about the African taken from the Internet. He was indeed a hero. There were photos of him with Bill Clinton, Nelson Mandela and even the Dalai Lama. He had even received a humanitarian award from Bill Gates. There were many articles about him surrounded by kids, him holding larger-than-life cheques in the thousands of dollars made out to something called the Never Again Foundation. I had heard of it before, Hollywood types were always appearing on TV appealing for donations, ending their

spiel with the now famous catchphrase, 'Not on my watch!'
It wasn't clear from the cuttings what Joshua's relationship
to the Foundation was – in some he was named as a founder,
in others as a past chairman – but whatever it was it seemed
like the man was at the centre of every good deed. And every
other do-gooder wanted a photo with him.

Initially, I was a little bitter – cops die every day without
as much as a nod from the powers that be – but reading on
I saw that he had earned every accolade he had received. A
former headmaster, he had turned his deserted school into
a safe haven during the Rwandan genocide. Revered by the
genocidaires, who were his former students, he had persuaded
them to let him and the school where they had once been
students alone. *An Island of Sanity In a Sea of Blood* one headline
screamed. He gave sanctuary to thousands, many of whom he
managed to smuggle over the border one way or another. But
at the height of the genocide his former students surrounded
the school and told him, 'No more in; no more out.' After this
those who tried to make it in were massacred.

This is where his story became even more remarkable.
During the siege he was only allowed to drive in and out
with a driver and a bodyguard, but this didn't stop him. He
ferried out two refugees at a time – disguised as his driver and
bodyguard – and smuggled them over the border to camps in
Tanzania and Kenya. On his way back to the school he would
then pick up two more of those trying to escape the violence
and dress them up as his driver and bodyguard.

What a story!

Now I could see why he was so calm in the face of the
white girl's death. It must have taken nerves of steel to pull

the same trick over and over again, risking not only his own life but also the lives of all those inside the school. He hadn't been exaggerating. He had lived with death, and a dead white girl on his doorstep was just one more dead amongst a million. Only the living would interest a man like him.

'You can find all that stuff online, but take the file,' the Chief said as we both stood up. 'Ishmael, we've been at this for a long time now, what does your gut tell you?' he asked after a pause.

In our world, this is not a light question. On the surface it meant we had nothing much to go by but underneath it meant that he was prepared to stick his neck out on my say. It's a rare question.

'He may be a hero somewhere in Africa, but he's mixed up in this shit somehow,' I said, remembering how I had drawn my gun – that was my gut speaking. 'It's simple, Chief, when was the last time a body landed on your doorstep from nowhere?'

'We have to get the son of a bitch who did this. You hear me?' he said fiercely. 'This is a little more than the department looking bad.'

I understood him. If we solved what was going to be a high-profile case, it would open more doors for black people in the force. And if we fucked up, other doors would close. It didn't make things any easier.

❮ Just as I stepped outside the Chief's door my cellphone rang. It was my contact at *The Madison Times*, a small ragtag tabloid that everybody read. Most cops, if they want to leak something, go to the big papers, but over the years I had learned that criminals, accomplices and those that wish them ill don't read the *Wisconsin State Journal*, and they certainly don't read *The New York Times*. If you want to get something back from your leak, get it to the small papers – everyone reads them. So I was glad it was Monique Shantell, or Mo as she preferred to be called, on the phone.

'Hey, Ishmael, you got something for me?' She sounded all sorts of sexy.

'Are you outside with the rest of them?' I asked.

'You know me, baby, I don't swim with the sharks. You must be ready for breakfast. Meet me at the usual place.'

The press looked up as I walked down the steps and convulsed towards me, realised I was not the Chief and went back to their chatter. For them, there were only two kinds of black people in the police station – those in handcuffs and the Chief.

I found Mo in my favourite little coffee shop, a few blocks from the station. I was a regular because they made the best coffee in Madison – milk, coffee, water and sugar boiled together for hours on end. Mo was beautiful and she knew it. She would never date me for the same reason that my wife had left me – I was a black cop and I sometimes arrested black people: I was a traitor to my race. At least that's what I told myself. I didn't like the alternative – that she just wasn't attracted to me.

'The shit will hit the fan with this one,' Mo said after I had given her a copy of the girl's Polaroid and a random story from the file the Chief had given me.

'Yeah, but you don't mind being in the trenches. Wear

them boots,' I teased her.

'You know something? It makes sense that he would kill her and leave her body right there,' she said with conviction.

'Why?' I asked. She had my attention.

'You're the detective, you tell me,' she said and laughed. 'Gotta run, babe, story to write, Pulitzer to win.' She stood up, leaned over and kissed me lightly on my mouth. That's how she kept my hopes alive. I didn't mind.

I stared at my coffee thinking about the legwork in front of me. Jesus, don't I hate it, but the devil is in the details as they say. So I went to the university and talked with Joshua's alibis – they had parted ways somewhere between half twelve and one am. The cops going through registration records had found nothing. The neighbours had seen nothing. No, there was nothing out of the ordinary about him. I went to motels around Madison: nothing. Missing person's files: nothing.

In the meantime the forensic search of Joshua's house had also produced nothing – and they had torn the place apart, even stripped his car. The Chief had then pulled Joshua's phone, credit card, and bank records, but even this move had failed to deliver any new information. Not only did the girl not exist, there was absolutely nothing to tie her to Joshua except that we had found her dead on his doorstep. By the end of that day, my only hope was that Mo's story would reveal a grieving parent, sibling, lover, or just someone who had served her some coffee – anyone who had seen her before she died.

❮ Mo's story broke the following day, but it didn't bring us any new information. Instead it made race relations much worse. Just the week before some Hmong guy had shot five white hunters, picking them off one by one. Afterwards he had said that they fired at him first, but how do you shoot five armed men in self-defence?

The Hmong guy was an immigrant, and here was another killing by an immigrant. It didn't matter that this immigrant was also a hero, and not just any hero but one who had saved hundreds from death in the middle of genocide. The KKK, led by a nasty-looking little man called James Wellstone, began mobilising its members from outlying farming towns to march across Madison and, according to their more radical members, lynch him. I had knocked some respect into James a couple of years earlier when he had entered my office yelling niggers this, niggers that after a white kid, a prep boy who loved his weed, had been beaten up in Allied Drive. And so when he came to the station to get a rally permit I did my best to talk him out of doing something stupid, but I knew that the best I could hope for was an uneasy peace.

Meanwhile, as I had expected, CNN, *The New York Times* and talk TV and Radio shows had picked up Mo's story – the same photograph being shown over and over again. In a few short hours the girl had come to represent all that was right and had gone wrong in America. The whites felt they were under siege; the black folk felt that white justice was going too far in incriminating Joshua.

To make it worse, the Mayor and Governor were coming down hard on the Chief, but not so hard as to rally the blacks against them. Politicians are masters of double speak. If the Mayor says that he 'trusts the Chief of Police will do all in his power to ensure that the right thing is done', to the whites it means that the Chief won't hesitate to hang a fellow black man if it comes down to it. To the blacks it means – don't forget who owns the police.

Only two days had gone by yet the dance was in full motion. The black leaders – Jesse Jackson-Al Sharpton-types – had crawled out of the woodwork for another fifteen minutes of fame, rallying around Joshua, calling him the black Schindler. The Mayor and Governor were guaranteeing results – hoping for a lifetime of white votes. Even the KKK had new recruits. Only one thing would remain unchanged – the white trailers, the black ghettoes and the cops holding down the lid so that nothing spilled into Maple Bluff.

I was getting angry and had to remind myself to stay focused. This was my job and I was going to follow the evidence wherever it led me. They say for each detective there is the one case that makes or breaks him or her. My training and my other cases had led me here. I would follow this path to whatever end. My reason was simple but immutable – it was wrong that someone had killed her and even more wrong for the killer to go free. My allegiance was to the dead white girl. She had died alone. No one had claimed her.

As the second day came to an end I still had nothing, not even her name. It's not that we hadn't tried everything. By that evening her clothes, her nail polish, her stomach contents – you name it – had gone through forensics. We had even managed to trace the trash from Maple Bluff to the dumping grounds and rummaged through it. And we still had nothing that would narrow her down from the millions of young women who shop in malls and occasionally eat a slice of pepperoni pizza.

❝ At eight o'clock that evening with nothing more to do, I decided to pay Joshua a visit. He was under heavy police protection, and I had to show my badge several times before finally knocking on his door. There was a uniform inside and he let me in, but to my surprise, I didn't find the same Joshua I had met just two nights earlier.

'I survived! I will not die here!' He was pacing up and down in his silk pyjamas, clearly agitated, in his hand a nearly empty bottle of red wine. He looked much thinner and much taller. 'Never again,' he said. 'Never again.'

He must have known that the MBPD cops were there to protect him from being lynched – he wasn't under arrest – but it didn't seem to matter to him. He had gone somewhere inside his own head, somewhere where what was happening around him made a different kind of sense, and when he looked at me it was without any sign of recognition. In fact, it was only once he had emptied the bottle of wine, and sent the cop to the wine cellar with the order 'Any year will do', that he looked at me like he knew who I was. 'Sit,' he commanded. I sat. 'We shall drink any year, all year and celebrate America, eh?' he asked sarcastically. 'You, I answer all your question with no warrant, eh? Why did you send police to search my home?' But before I could answer he said, to no one in particular, 'But I understand. You similar, like all of them … You only follow order, no?'

His accent was heavier than it had been when we had first met. Just how much wine had he had? I wondered as the cop, a bit winded by the stairs, returned with a bottle. Joshua took it and expertly knocked the neck against the edge of the table so that it broke off cleanly, then he poured himself a full glass.

'And my guest?' he asked the cop, who went to the kitchen and came back with another wine glass. 'Good day when whites serve blacks, no?' he said with a mean laugh as the cop, red in the face, returned.

As Joshua poured me a full glass I decided that I would follow his lead, treading carefully. He was drunk, not stupid. He needed to talk. I would listen.

'Ishmael, you know what it mean to die?' he asked.

I shook my head.

'It mean nothing. Nothing unless you live. Paradox. Survivor like me know death. You ever kill, Ishmael?' he asked.

'Yes,' I answered truthfully. But this was Madison – so not often. And the few times that I had shot anyone, I had ended up throwing up. I had come to understand it was to purge myself. Not that I slept any better for it. 'And you, Joshua, have you ever taken a life?' I asked him.

'Genocide, no game.' He wagged a long finger from side to side. 'No hide and seek, no police and robbers. I … I traded lives, Ishmael. Now tell no lie, eh? You ever save one life, two life, three life, hundred of life, more than a thousand life?' He looked at me and laughed.

'No,' I said.

'When you deal big, you trade big. You read me? I big hero, no?'

'Yes,' I said.

'A million dead. You compare that to thousand I save. I trade losing hand, no?'

'Look, man, we do what we can. You were only one man. Without you it would have been a million plus one thousand.

We do what we can. I do what I can. The girl is dead, but I would rather have saved her than catch the killer,' I said earnestly.

'You speak like friend to me. But no, man, you trade small; a life here, a life there. When you trade big, you lose big. No winner.' He paused and looked at me, and for a moment his eyes were sober. 'Detective Ishmael, why you here?'

I thought I could see an opening. 'Why was there a dead white girl outside your house?' I asked.

'We are here. Me and you. Man to man. Ask what you want, no? Tomorrow, who remember?' I heard the cop in the room shuffle his feet uncomfortably.

'Did you kill the girl?' I asked, my heart racing. Any confession he gave would be thrown out of court – the suspect was shit-faced – but at least I would know, and once I knew I could work my way backwards.

'Wrong question. Start from beginning,' he said with laugher in his voice, as if he could sense my desperation.

It was too late to do anything else, so I went on the offensive. 'Look here, Joshua, you might be some sort of hero, but in this country they won't think twice about taking your life for the girl's,' I said, trying to sound sincere. 'You're a nigger here, like me or the guy they shot forty-one times in New York.'

'Your shield no protect you,' he said. 'I hear what happen in New York.'

It still made me angry to think about it. Damn it, a black undercover agent shot dead by two white cops in New York. How does one explain that?

'But, still, I never meet her,' Joshua continued. 'Why kill

somebody I never meet?' He shrugged his shoulders. 'Ishmael, let me tell you something. You say me and you niggers, but you do not know what you say. You want African and you to be nigger? You desire brotherhood of pain?' he asked, his voice full of concern.

'What are you talking about, Joshua?' I asked him.

'I show you what I mean,' he announced, standing up and suddenly stomping his naked foot onto the broken neck of the wine bottle. He trembled in pain, then, reaching down, he pulled the neck from his foot. Blood gushed out, and he threw the bloody shard towards me.

'You desire brotherhood of pain ... ? Now you do it,' he yelled.

I stared back at him calmly. This was a test of will. I knew playing along would not earn his respect but neither would walking away.

'Now that was foolish,' I finally said.

'Ishmael! Your turn!' he commanded.

'If you want to torture me, play me some of that African music,' I said as calmly as I could and reached out to pour myself some more wine from the neckless bottle.

Joshua smiled. 'I like you, Ishmael', he said.

Hobbling over to his entertainment centre, trailing blood across the floor, Joshua pulled out a turntable and put on some reggae. 'Alpha Blondie,' he explained.

I didn't wait for the first song to end before I chugged my wine. 'No ambulances, too much press out there, just get your kit,' I instructed the pillar of a cop as I got to the door.

'And another bottle,' Joshua yelled above the music.

❮ Walking down his driveway to my car I thought there were two possibilities. Either Joshua was lying and he had killed the girl or he really didn't know her and she was a message, a conversation between him and God knew whom. But I was convinced that he was part of the puzzle, if not the solution.

I made it back home in time for some late night TV. As I sat in my lounge I wondered what it means for an African to meet an African American. Joshua was the first African I had really interacted with. Sad to say, but that was the truth – most come to Madison for school and leave as soon as they're done. And those who stay are looking for the American dream – and part of achieving that is staying away from us.

Well, Joshua was my suspect. In another world, where the girl didn't exist, we probably wouldn't have met – me a struggling black cop and he an African hero. No point thinking about it, I told myself as I opened a cold Bud.

I was just about to open my second can of beer when my cellphone rang. 'Is this Detective Ishmael?' a voice with a heavy accent asked.

'Yes, that's me,' I answered and quickly looked for the caller's number. *Unknown*. It must have been an international number.

'If you want the truth, you must go to its source. The truth is in the past. Come to Nairobi.' And with that the person on the other end of the line hung up.

Almost immediately the phone rang again. 'Who is this?' I asked hurriedly.

'I see you got the call.' It was Mo. 'What did he want?'

'He wants me to go Africa.'

'Where?'

'Africa, goddamn it, fucking Africa …' I said, getting angry with Mo for no good reason.

'You gotta go,' she said. 'Babe, you have to.'

I wanted to see her. I asked if I could come over but she said no.

'Keep 'em coming, all right, baby?' she said and then she hung up.

I opened my beer. I finally had a lead. But what the hell? Who wanted to chase this thing all the way back to Africa? Where would I even start? But thinking back over the last two days, the call was only confirming what I had known instinctively: that, somehow, Joshua was in the middle of it.

❮ 'All that was last week,' I told O. 'I had to plead with the Chief to give me two weeks. After two weeks I told him that he could throw me to the wolves if I didn't have something for him. No one besides you, your Chief and my Chief knows I'm here. If the press in the United States finds out that the lead investigator is chasing ghosts in Africa, it's off with our heads. So, O, that's how come I'm sitting with you here drinking Tusker beer and eating *nyama choma* instead of solving my case.'

'Damn, Ishmael!' O whistled through his teeth. 'What a story, what a story. So you are here because of a single telephone call? The suspect and the victim are back in your country and you are here? And you do not even know who called your ass?'

I couldn't help laughing with him at the absurdity of the situation.

'It is crazy but somehow it makes sense,' O finally said. 'But tonight we drink, eat and make merry for tomorrow we die ... Cheers!'

And suddenly, for the night, we were just two cops working a case that was bigger than us, sharing one, two, many beers. Sometimes it's good to take a day off so that you can start the next day with fresh eyes.

It had taken about two hours to fill O in. Soon after I had finished my story a man walked into the bar carrying a guitar. He and the bartender yelled back and forth for a while. He had been supposed to come at ten, O explained, for 'one man guitar'. I was very tired, ready for sleep, but I didn't want to leave before hearing some music.

As the man finally made his way to the stage I noticed that I was breathing hard and that my hands had balled themselves into fists. I felt incredibly anxious, as if my life depended on the music that this man would play – it was as if I was on the verge of a panic attack. Then, without any introduction or fanfare, the man looked straight at me and said in halting English, 'This, for my black brother. Remember black brother, tip bartender and I well.'

His small speech over he started tapping the guitar with his hands so that the sound came at the tail of his laughter. He sounded like a one-man drum machine. And then he stopped, so that the silence in the bar almost became a song – the soft mutterings of the drunks, the hot wind blowing through the doorway, the sound of teeth tearing meat from bones and the clatter of glasses and bottles. I felt like I was being lifted out of myself, but before I was completely gone sounds that were half blues and half something else brought me back. His hands were a blur, his feet furiously tapping dust high into the air as the yellowish light from the kerosene lamp bathed him in a golden glow.

The bartender walked over and stood in front of the guitar player. She started moving slowly – so slowly that she seemed to be pulling against the furious rhythm, a tug of war that she was slowly losing so that her hips and arms flailed faster and faster until it looked like she was being jerked around by the music. Then, just when it started looking painful, the guitar slowed down to a familiar blues melody – one note at a time, one tap at a time. It was the guitar pulling her back to earth as she slowly gyrated to the ground. Then, just as suddenly as it had begun, the song ended and the bartender clapped her hands and went back to the bar as if nothing had happened.

I started choking, having hardly breathed throughout the performance, but O seemed not to have noticed anything. I felt exhausted. I had been to a place within myself that I didn't know existed, a place that was beautiful and terrifying. The music had briefly awoken something in me – a rage or a healing. It was as if I had taken a hit of acid. Perhaps the beers and long plane ride, the jet lag and the exhaustion of the last few days had come to a head.

'Buy him a Tusker,' O said as he pushed a five hundred shilling note into my hand, 'if you liked the music, that is.'

'I'll pay you back when I change some money,' I said, but he simply waved me on drunkenly.

'Tonight no need for a hotel. Just crash at my place.' He took a photograph out of his wallet. 'Detective Ishmael, meet my wife,' he announced.

It was a rough photograph and I couldn't make out her

features beyond a small Afro. 'She's beautiful,' I said.

I waved the bartender over and gave her the money, gesturing a beer for her and the guitarist. 'Ten Tuskers?' she asked, lifting up ten fingers.

I laughed. 'Why not?'

As we were leaving, she was piling the bottles at the guitarist's feet. 'Goodbye, my black brother,' the guitarist said, with a deep laugh, nodding his head back and forth to the music he was playing.

I waved. 'Goodbye, black brother,' I repeated.

Neither a tourist nor a visitor, but a detective in search of the truth – and not just any detective, a black American detective – I knew I was about to enter Africa's underbelly. If lucky, I would see some beauty as well. But as we left The Hilton Hotel bar I knew I was not going to see Africa like some tourist staring at animals through a pair of binoculars.

WHERE DREAMS COME TO DIE

« We got to O's place really late. He lived in Eastleigh Estate, which he described as a lower-middle class Nairobi suburb. Lit by the Land Rover's headlights the houses all looked the same – narrow, two-storey dwellings with chain-link fences and fierce-looking dogs – and with all the twists and turns, it felt like we were tunnelling through a maze. Eventually we arrived at his house, where he showed me to an empty room. Within minutes I was fast asleep.

O shook me awake just before dawn. After a cold shower I walked into the kitchen to find his wife sitting at the table grading hand-written papers – O hadn't told me she was a high school teacher. Of medium height, and a little bit on the stocky side, she was wearing a long black-and-white polka-dotted dress and sported a huge Afro. She reminded me of photos I had seen of black women in the 1960s – the radical feminists with a fist always up in the air. She had a gap between her two front teeth, the only flaw in an otherwise perfect smile.

'My name is Maria, Odhiambo's wife,' she said, pointing

33

to O, who was busy making breakfast.

I introduced myself and watched as she gathered her papers together, finished her cup of tea and kissed O goodbye.

O was quite a chef – his omelette was superb. 'It is because you Americans use frozen ingredients. Here it is straight from the garden,' he said when I complimented him. Then he smiled. 'And my wife cannot cook. She tries but she is not gifted that way.'

'You are a rare breed, my friend,' I said, much to his delight. 'A black male feminist detective chef.'

He took a joint from his shirt pocket. 'Now I am a black male feminist detective chef with a joint,' he said as he lit up.

I don't smoke weed, not because I'm a cop, it's just that it gives me the giggles – hours of ridiculous, uncontrollable laughter – and I would rather not look stupid.

'Today we will rattle the bushes,' O said after I had declined a drag on his joint.

He and I both knew that if the man who had told me to come to Nairobi was serious all we had to do was show up in the right places, make our presence known, and he would find us.

The first bush we rattled was the Rwandan Consulate. The consulate was in Muthaiga Estate, where the houses were so huge that I felt like I was back in Maple Bluff. Nothing. Of course they knew Joshua. Without people like him there would be no Rwanda. Could he have been involved in any criminal activities? No, of course not. Enemies? Yes. Could they be more specific? It could be anyone.

We went next to the Refugee Centre in Nairobi CBD, the charitable arm of the Never Again Foundation. The office was on the top floor with a magnificent view over the whole city. As we waited for the Director to see us I let my eyes wander out to the horizon, watching as the buildings got smaller and smaller and the smokestacks rose higher and higher above them.

After a fifteen-minute wait, we were let in to see the Director, Samuel Alexander, a white American dressed in a T-shirt and faded blue jeans. His office looked like some kind of African museum – from the artwork to the thick jungle plants – but he seemed very happy to see a fellow American, and for a few minutes he spoke about the things that he missed the most: McDonald's, fifty-two TV channels with nothing on them, high-speed Internet and the roads. 'By God, do I miss the roads,' he cried. 'The roads here are shit.' He had a point there, I concurred.

'So, gentlemen, what can I do for you?' Samuel Alexander finally asked.

I explained we were looking for information on Joshua – anything that might help us with an investigation we were conducting.

'About that white girl?' he asked. 'Courtesy of CNN International,' he added, seeing the look on my face.

'Yes,' I answered.

'The man is a *fucking* hero,' he said, stressing the word. He then asked us to go with him to a conference room and there we found several large posters of Joshua hanging on the wall covered with slogans like *You can be a hero too – give* and *I saved hundreds – so can you*. There were some brochures on the desk that also had his face on them. Joshua was their poster boy – his face helped them raise money, Samuel explained. It was

Samuel who had recruited Joshua shortly after the genocide to help with raising money for the Refugee Centre. But that was the extent of their relationship.

'Did you meet him here, in Nairobi?' I asked him.

'Yes, several times. I gotta tell you though, Joshua is a gentle African ... He would never harm anyone,' he answered.

Finally, I asked Samuel Alexander if he knew of any Rwandan refugees or genocide survivors that we could talk to, but he told me that it would be a privacy breach to give us such information.

As we took the lift back down to the ground floor I was happy that we had at least placed Joshua in Nairobi. Beyond that we had nothing, but it didn't matter, we were rattling the bushes.

Later, as we ate a lunch of fried chicken and fries, O told me that he had an idea of where we could find some Rwandan refugees. He suggested we leave his Land Rover in the city – in his car we would be easily made – and take public transport to a place called Mathare.

After we were done eating, O flagged down a small rainbow-coloured Nissan matatu that had Tupac's 'Dear Mama' playing at full volume. We got off in Mathare – a slum area – and stood on the side of the tarmac road, trying to decide which of the muddy footpaths that wove in and out of the endless rows of shacks we should take. It was as if I had stepped into one of those infomercials with the stream of skeletal children, too used to the flies crawling over their faces to shoo them away. And the smell – it was a surprise. In spite of the open sewers and the thousands of barely clothed sweating bodies milling around us it wasn't a bad smell. Yes, it had several layers to it – sex, shit, cheap perfume, bad breath, booze, weed, sickness – but the sum of these parts wasn't bad, and though it settled in my throat like thick smoke, it didn't make me cough.

O explained that Mathare was sectioned off into various ethnicities – you had the Luo, Kikuyu and Kamba sections. And then you had the refugee section, itself sectioned off according to nationality – Sudanese, Ugandan, Congolese, et cetera. This was a land of suffering, an inverted Tower of Babel that descended into hell instead of rising to heaven.

We made our rounds – O, with his spare frame and bloodshot eyes, almost fitting in; me, with my American baby fat, sticking out – until we found the Rwandan section. 'We are from the Refugee Centre and would like to talk to you,' O would say as he knocked on one of the poles that held up the piece of sackcloth that the residents used as a door. Then we would show Joshua's photograph to the occupants, but everyone we asked just looked back at us and said they didn't know him.

After three hours of house-to-house I was starving. O spotted some small boys roasting maize over a fire, went over and negotiated for two full cobs. Used to American corn, I took a huge bite only to find it so hard I thought my front teeth would break. One of the boys laughed, took the cob from me and showed me how to shell it, holding it with his left hand and picking at it with his right. He said something to me in Kiswahili.

'He is saying this is tax,' O translated as the boy threw the pieces he had shelled up in the air in quick succession, leaning back, mouth open so that they landed on his tongue. Then he handed my cob back and we were off, leaving him and his friends beside themselves with laughter.

Peeling one kernel at a time it took me what seemed like forever to finish my snack, but finish it I did. However, as I threw the empty cob away I heard a woman screaming from somewhere nearby. I looked around, but everybody was going on about his or her business as if deaf to the sound. For a moment I thought I was hearing things.

'Follow me, Ishmael,' O said urgently, moving in the opposite direction to the noise. 'Remember where you are,' he warned.

I took a step after O and the woman screamed; another step, another scream. I felt like she could see me abandoning her and I couldn't stand it. Turning, I started walking back towards the screams, then broke into a full run with my gun drawn, people jumping out of my way.

Guided by her voice, I ran until I was outside one of the shacks. Pulling back the cloth that hung across the door, I made out the shape of a man, with his pants rolled to his knees, lying on top of the screaming girl. I walked in quietly, letting the curtain fall back into place, and stuck my gun to the man's head. He must have thought it was a friend playing a joke on him because he said something in Kiswahili, laughed and made as if to continue with the rape. 'Motherfucker,' I said as I slid the safety off.

He stopped immediately and rolled off the girl, trying desperately to pull up his pants and put up his hands at the same time. O came in, and without asking any questions knocked the man to the ground and handcuffed him. Meanwhile the girl, in a white-and-red school uniform, had rolled down her skirt and was desperately trying to button her torn blouse. 'Are you learning English in school?' I asked her.

She nodded.

'What's your name?'

'Janet,' she whispered.

'Okay, Janet, I promise we'll get you out of here,' I said, trying to sound gentle, surprised at how calm I was.

O hadn't said a word but I could tell he was furious. Then he seemed to make up his mind about something and sprang into action. He handed Janet his jacket, walked to the makeshift door and looked outside. Moving back into the shack he stuck a dirty sock in the man's mouth, pulled him to his feet and, holding him by the seat of his pants, gun held to the back of his head, he pushed him outside. Janet and I followed, my Glock held firmly in front of me.

A crowd had formed outside, but it parted to let us through. We didn't know where we were, so O asked the girl, and she pointed us in the direction we needed to go. With Janet guiding us it wasn't long before we saw headlights rushing past on the road up ahead, but just when I thought we were in the clear, I heard someone yell something behind us in Kiswahili. It sounded like a command, and we turned around to see four young men dressed like they had just popped out of a rap video, only instead of fistfuls of dollars their hands held AK-47s and they were aiming them at us. It was then that I understood what I had done. It was as if my partner and I had gone to Allied Drive without backup, arrested a gang leader, and then tried to walk him out on foot.

I pushed Janet behind me as a thin trickle of cold sweat

ran down my neck. It was simple, we were going to die here, I thought as I pointed the Glock in the general direction of the young men.

O was standing with the rapist in front of him, holding his gun to the back of his head. He said something to the men and they hissed back at us. If we let the rapist go they would kill us anyway. I asked O to tell them we would trade their friend if they let the girl go. Nothing doing.

'You got us into this,' a voice inside me was yelling as I looked around desperately, trying to figure out how we were going to get out of the mess I had managed to dump us in. Then it came to me. I suddenly realised that we could see the thugs a lot better than they could see us – we had our backs to the road, which meant that each time a car came past its headlights dazzled them. I looked across at O as the next car whizzed by, then I looked back at the men. O nodded that he understood and immediately I started yelling all sorts of motherfuckers at them. They were amused for a few seconds, and then they shouted something at O, training their guns on the girl and me. They couldn't shoot O without killing their man, but they could kill us both easily. A second or so later another car came by and O shot the rapist.

Unless you're well trained, the sound of a gunshot will make you freeze. A seasoned thug will react just like a cop and shoot back instinctively, but these young men were clearly not in that category. They froze for a half-second, maybe even less, shocked by the sound of the gun and the sight of their friend's blood, illuminated by the headlights, spraying into the sky.

As the rapist lurched forward I turned and pushed Janet

down so that we both fell to the earth. I rolled once, and while still on the ground I aimed for a split second and fired, aimed again and fired again. Two of the young men flailed in the air before going down. O hadn't missed either, and only their leader managed to get a couple of rounds off, his bullets kicking around us harmlessly, before O dropped him too.

The shooting over, we secured the scene. Three of the thugs had been fatally wounded but the leader was still alive. He started to say something, making pleading gestures, but O shot him twice – once in the heart and once in the head. I walked a few feet from the bodies, bent over and threw up, my fear, shock and disgust adding to the thick stench of humanity in Mathare.

« After the shootout O had called his station and within minutes a car arrived to pick us up. I had fully expected that we would be interrogated by the CID equivalent of internal affairs as soon as we got back to the station, then we would have to fill out mountains of paperwork before being sent to a review board and hauled to a psych consult, but I was wrong.

'You are in good shape, the criminals are dead and the young woman is still alive. Be off, gentlemen,' the Director of Investigations, a rather young-looking man, had said to us. It was almost as if we had never been to Mathare and left five young men dead.

After our debriefing we took Janet to Kenyatta National Hospital and stayed with her while they ran all sorts of tests. We had been expecting the worst, but when the doctor finally walked out of Janet's room her face told a different story.

'Thank God, the semen does not have traces of HIV. She will be okay,' she said.

Relieved, we walked into Janet's room to find her in tears. She was dressed in a hospital gown and O's jacket – her school uniform, socks and shoes in the metal trashcan in the corner. O walked over to her and hugged her. We both knew that her ordeal was only really just beginning, but there was nothing more we could do for her. There were psychiatrists in Nairobi, but she would never be able to afford them. Her only choice was to return to school as if nothing had happened.

'Where do you go to school?' O asked her.

She went to Loreto Convent, Msongari.

'Isn't that a boarding school?'

'I am on bursary,' she answered.

It turned out that Janet's mother had died in the Rwandan genocide, and she lived with her father in Mathare – she walked home every day as her scholarship didn't cover her boarding fees.

O went out and returned moments later with a dress and slippers – 'From one of the nurses,' he explained. Then, together, we left the hospital and went to a nearby café. We were starving, and in spite of our various traumas we ate like we hadn't seen a meal in a week. Afterwards, we took Janet to her school, where O explained what had happened to a stern-looking black sister in a habit and wimple. Janet had two more years to go and was a bright girl, she told us. She would see to it that she was allowed to board.

We drove back to Eastleigh Estate without much conversation. It was late in the evening, almost midnight by the time we arrived at O's place and his wife had already gone to bed. He walked me to my room and stood in the doorway as I plopped onto the bed, feeling weightless and empty.

'We traded five lives for one,' I said to him, thinking of my conversation with Joshua.

I didn't mean anything by it. The words just came out of my mouth. What choice did we have? I could not pretend that I couldn't hear Janet's screams. We couldn't have let the thugs kill us either. But still, it was five lives for one. Once I decided to help Janet, I had set the wheels in motion – people were going to die.

'Better the bad guys than the good guys, I suppose,' I added.

'Ishmael, me and you, we are not good people. We have done some good and some bad … But Janet is a good person and she survived. That cannot be a bad thing,' O said as he pulled the door shut.

A few minutes later I heard the shower start running, and, exhausted, I drifted off to sleep.

« *I was a bird – flying, dipping in and out of clouds – then suddenly I became a huge plane carrying white tourists, then I was rushing into a kitchen because something was burning only to find a canister of tear gas in the oven. I looked away, to see if I could find my wife, and when I looked back the canister became a birthday cake, and my wife and I were each cutting a piece. But when I was just about to take a bite, I saw that instead of a cake, it was a human heart – still beating even with us holding pieces of it that looked like cake. I tried to warn my wife but she couldn't hear me. I had lost my voice. She took a bite and the whole heart quivered …*

I woke up at five am and decided to take a walk. Outside, the morning air was crisp and slightly stale. In the light of the sun, yellowish through the mist, Eastleigh looked peaceful and even the piles of garbage along the tarmacked streets looked somehow beautiful. A few blocks past O's house, I saw little children in clean blue-and-white uniforms closing a metal gate behind them. They were yawning and I couldn't help smiling. I said hello to them, but they looked at me suspiciously. I continued on.

Close to a shopping centre, I saw old Somali women putting up their makeshift stalls, bales of fresh mangoes, bananas and khat waiting to be displayed. At the bus station, bus and matatu drivers were readying their vehicles for a busy morning. Loud music – a confused mix of different rap songs – was playing above the roar of backfiring engines. I walked on.

At a kiosk, I bought some tea and a chapatti. I sat on a bench blowing the hot chai steam into the air to cool it down. Nobody paid me any attention – this early in the morning people were busy minding their own stories.

I thought back to how, once, in New Jersey investigating one thing or another, I was talking to this old man and it came out that he had never been to New York. New York, a thirty-minute train ride from Newark! 'I have no reason to go to New York,' he'd said with a shrug. Then it had seemed odd, that not even curiosity would get him onto that train, but now, somehow, I understood. If you have everything you need where you are, why go somewhere else? That was how I felt about being in Africa. Until the dead white girl had shown up on Joshua's doorstep, I had never had a reason to come to

Africa. And so I hadn't.

A little pickup truck with *Daily Nation* written all over it slowed down briefly and a man in the back threw a plastic covered bundle in the general direction of the door to the kiosk. It landed in a puddle of filth. The owner cursed, came out with a knife and opened it up. I watched him idly arranging the newspapers on his makeshift stand, adding cigarettes and Wrigley's gum to the display. But just when I was about to go back to my tea and thoughts, the headline caught my eye: *The Case of the Dead White Girl: American Detective in Kenya*.

Immediately, I went to pick up the newspaper, but the man asked for money first. I rummaged through my wallet but I had spent the last of my Kenyan shillings on the chai and chapatti and smallest bill I could find was a ten. I gave it to him, wondering whether he would accept it. He held it up in the air, looked at it for a few seconds. 'American money ... very good,' he finally said approvingly and pushed the newspaper into my hand.

My anxiety grew as I began to read the lead story. It was all there: how the girl had been found, how she had no identity, her photograph (the headshot of her lifeless body in full colour), my name, everything except my photograph. But even that was surely only a matter of time. This was going to change things, and for the worse I suspected. I needed to talk with the Chief.

I gulped down my tea and made to leave, but the kiosk owner grabbed my arm and pressed into my hand a small plastic bag full of chapattis, bread and sodas. He waved the ten dollar bill and pointed to the bag. I had bought the stuff. I smiled, touched, and shook my head, thrusting the plastic bag back into his hands. I didn't have time to argue. I had to get back to O's.

❮ 'Look, man, this is the break we have been waiting for,' O said, beside himself with excitement. Unlike in the United States most Kenyans read the paper, and if they don't, they listen to the radio, so O figured that something was bound to come up.

I had tried calling the Chief but I couldn't get through – I didn't have enough airtime. O suggested that I text the Chief and ask him to call me back. I was sceptical, but it worked fine because a few minutes later the phone rang.

'Chief, I'm staring at the local paper, where are my two weeks?' I asked, stressing each word.

'Too much pressure ... Everyone wanted to know where we are with the case. We have nothing here, and I had to throw them something. What the hell could I do? I told them you had left for Africa, that we were onto something big ... ' He paused and I knew that he was waiting for me to tell him we had something.

'Chief, I only just got here ... ' I started.

'Listen, you've got one week,' the Chief said, interrupting me. 'You'd better have something in a week, otherwise we're dead in the water ... Don't let us down, Ishmael.'

I started to protest, but he had already hung up.

I went back to the kitchen to find O making breakfast – the exact same breakfast as the day before. 'I perfect one meal a year, so for a year that is all I cook, no deviations, no nothing, the same exact thing each time until I get it right,' he said when he saw the look on my face. 'I have been working on this masterpiece since January …'

I laughed at the idea – it made sense. 'What do we do now?' I asked as I poured myself some coffee.

O produced a joint from behind his ear. 'We smoke, then we eat a *motherfucking* omelette,' he said, trying to sound like he was from the hood.

'You have a way with words, my friend, you know that? You scared those motherfuckers with your motherfuckers last night. I did not know you spoke black American.' He laughed in delight.

O slipped in and out of Americanisms easily – Americanisms that had filtered into Kenyan culture through movies and music videos. And he did it fluidly because he wasn't self-conscious about it. I, on the other hand, brought up by black middle-class parents, had been trained from an early age to disdain colloquialisms – Ebonics was forbidden. That was a long time ago, but rightly or wrongly I was brought up believing that to make it in the United States black people had to speak proper American English. The change in my diction had obviously surprised O.

After breakfast – just as good as the previous day's – I went to the bathroom for a shower. I waited for the water to run hot, but I was out of luck – a cold shower again. Back in my room I put on jeans, sneakers and a T-shirt and grabbed a light jacket which would easily hide my gun when I put it on.

As soon as I walked back into the kitchen, O pulled out a deck of cards. The only game we both knew was Crazy Eights – a rather childish game, but there was nothing more to do except wait. We played one long hand and then gave up.

Every cop hates down time. It's the worst. It feels like the rest of the world knows something you don't, and everything that is not related to the case feels like an interruption, but there is nothing to do except wait. O was a talker, so we sat around shooting the breeze for a while, trying to keep our minds off the waiting game.

'Your wife, tell me about your wife,' he finally said.

What the hell, I thought, it was as good a time as any to get into the personal stuff. 'Childhood sweetheart. We grew into each other ... Know what I mean? Broke up several times, but kept coming back for more. So, we got married,' I said, trying to sound flippant.

'And then you grew apart?' O asked.

'That's it. I don't know how it is being a cop around here, but back in the States being black and a cop has some ... complications. She said she couldn't stand my being a cop. The truth is our paths drifted further and further apart. By the time she was getting her MBA, I was getting my badge; she went corporate, I went to the streets. You know what I mean? My street life didn't jive with her ambitions ... Finally, I think she just stopped loving me. Perhaps we never stood a chance from the beginning.'

Did I miss her? Hell yeah, and the more she couldn't stand me the more I wanted her. The more life in the streets took stuff out of me, the more I needed her. '"You want to consume me!" Those were her last words to me,' I said to O.

It takes a long time to be fair to your ex. I had thought it had been long enough, but the bitterness with which I had spoken suggested otherwise.

'Listen, man,' O said, sounding stoned, 'I know just what

you mean. Last night I wanted to consume my wife … ' He paused. 'What a beautiful word: consume.' He let the word roll off his tongue a few more times.

'I think, at the end of it all, my wife hated me, and that was one of the hardest things to accept,' I continued, feeling that now I had started my confession I had to get it all out in the open. 'I couldn't reconcile myself to the fact that over the years she developed a basic contempt for me and found my work petty. "A simple man after simple truths," she liked to say at the end of every argument.' I paused and looked up into O's bloodshot eyes. 'I knew things were coming to an end when she started giving me this look. I had never seen it before, and I can't really describe it, but it contained a fucked-up mix of contempt, resentment, self-loathing and love. I mean, she would bite her lip and look deep into my eyes as if she was trying to tell me something telepathically … It was creepy.'

'Shit, man, you should have just asked her what she was trying to tell you,' O said.

'Yeah, I suppose, but I was going through my own shit: at work, with my parents. I was growing up. I didn't know how to ask. Do you know what I mean?'

O gave me that blank look of his. 'No, I do not know what you mean. You gotta ask … Always ask,' he said with conviction and took a deep drag on his joint.

'I'll get them to put that on your tombstone,' I said. 'Detective O: always ask.'

'And what does she do now?'

'She works for Shell … Runs their business offices in New York. Good for her, I guess.'

'You have to appreciate this here irony,' O said, trying his American accent again. 'Look, man, Shell is busy fucking Africa and she thinks you are the bad guy 'cos you are a black cop? See what I mean?' He had this look of satisfaction on his face, like he had just relieved me of a great burden. He was high. I wasn't.

'Jesus, O! This shit is too heavy for breakfast. Let's save it for a drunken night,' I said, standing up and starting to pace up and down. 'Fucking down time! We need something to do. I'm going crazy.'

'My wife and I, we have rules, man,' O said, looking contemplative. 'I come home and have to be a husband, no matter what. I have to leave my work right at that door. Maria says, "I don't treat you like a kid, so don't treat me like a criminal." Don't get me wrong, I mean, I can still tell her about my day and some of the shit that goes down, but I can't break dishes and throw things around. I'm not allowed to take it out on her. It might seem strange to you, but shit works, man ...'

Did my ex and I have such rules, even unspoken ones? In true American spirit we wanted everything examined, laid out on the table and talked about – family time, we called it. But surely a marriage has to have a dark basement that no one goes to – where some things are thrown and left to rot because they are toxic? Maybe what my wife and I had needed were secrets?

'Why did you decide to become a cop?' I asked O, changing tack. Everyone wants to know why people are who they are – and more so with cops. The question really is: What made you dumb enough to risk your life for a head full of bad dreams, a failed marriage and no pay?

'There was only one university in the whole country back in the day. I didn't get in. It was either this, join the army or become a criminal,' O said, sounding as if everyone in Kenya had faced the same choices.

Why had I become a cop? I had talked about it often enough to have a prepared answer – wanting to do some good – but the actual reasons were more complex. I had gone to college, graduated with a useless degree that I could only have turned into a living by getting my PhD and becoming a professor … But the boredom! I did not want to become a drone, reciting the same lectures from ten years earlier about the US Constitution – although that's exactly what my parents wanted for me.

My father worked as an accountant and my mother taught at a community college. I was an only child, and on their combined salaries we had lived well. I didn't join the force because it was the only way to get out of poverty. I was a rebel. I didn't want to become part of the black middle class with aspirations of whiteness – piano lessons and debutante balls. I had seen that world and didn't like it one little bit, so I had opted out and become a cop. So, even though my ex-wife thought I was a traitor to my race, to my mind I was more of myself than I would ever have been being black on someone else's terms. A paradox, but then what in life isn't?

'I didn't want to join the black middle class,' I answered O. 'It's true, I'm not out there fighting the man, but I do something,' I added.

'That's 'cos you are the man,' O said and laughed.

Just as I was about to call O a choice word, his phone

started ringing. He grinned from ear to ear. We both knew this was the call. It had to be.

'This had better not be my lovely wife,' he said as he answered. I was beside myself with curiosity, but O's face told me only that it was bad news – his jaw tense. 'Shit, he wants to talk to you,' he finally said, handing the phone over to me.

'O and I go a long way back. Tell him Lord Thompson wants to see you. Young man, I promise not to waste your time,' an old voice said before the line went dead.

'This cannot be good,' O said as he put out his joint and dabbed his eyes with cold water, 'but we have to go. Shit, I will have to do the dishes later.'

Down time hadn't been too bad, all things considered – it was still only one pm.

LORD THOMPSON

❝We drove away from Nairobi and headed into the farmlands. Outside of the city the roads were just as bad – if not worse – and just as in Nairobi the hawkers crowded around us at each massive pothole trying to sell us cigarettes, roasted corn and newspapers that screamed *The Case of the Dead White Girl: American Detective in Kenya*.

'Imagine this,' O said, trying to explain what Lord Thompson was like, 'what if a white slave owner convinced himself he was a slave and then tried to live like one?'

'You mean he became an abolitionist?' I asked.

'No, everything remains the same except that he actually lives like a slave,' he said as if I was missing the most obvious point in the world.

'He becomes a slave by choice?'

O finally gave up. 'No, man. You know what, let's just get there,' he said, the frustration in his voice plain. 'You have to see this shit for yourself. Then you will understand.'

After an hour of driving the road turned abruptly into a bumpy dirt track and almost immediately the landscape also changed. Where, before, the vegetation had been a thick luscious green, here, long dry grass that looked ready for a fire was interspersed with short dusty thickets of thirsty looking trees.

Thirty or so minutes later we turned off the main road onto another, smaller dirt track and not long after that the scenery changed once again. After the desolation we had just driven through I wasn't prepared for the plush oasis that suddenly surrounded me. The trees were green, the vegetation once again lush and the well-maintained road lined with rose bushes, their red blooms in stark contrast to the white stones that were spaced out between them. Even more incredible was that the road continued for close to three miles.

'Camouflage ...' O muttered to himself. 'This is how they hide. You would never think to look for them here.'

'Who?'

'The rich whites,' O answered. 'They prefer to remain invisible, so they create islands like this one.'

'Why?'

'History, man, history. It's the deal. After colonialism, they were supposed to remain invisible, and we were supposed to forget what they did,' O said bitterly. 'So they hide out in places like this.'

I didn't quite understand what he meant and didn't have time to ask – we had arrived at the gate.

After O had shown his badge to the guards on the gate we were allowed to make our way along the final few hundred metres of what was now a tarmacked road to emerge in front of what was undoubtedly the most gratuitously sized house I had ever seen – it wasn't a house, it was a presidential palace.

How could a man who lived like a slave live in a house like this? O had been right: I had to see for myself.

Having parked O's battered Land Rover on the expanse of gravel in front of the house we made our way up the red-carpeted stairs, many of them, until we got to the enormous front door. Once there O pulled a rope which rang what sounded like a giant bell somewhere deep inside the house, and moments later two Africans dressed in white shirts and shorts rolled back the huge oak doors.

We were led through spacious, elegant rooms – the kind I had only seen in catalogues (not even Maple Bluff compared) – before, finally, we came to a room that had two white guards in front it – AK-47s, full battle regalia, you name it.

'South African mercenaries,' O whispered.

They looked every bit the cliché: muscled, bearded and tattooed – they could have been cardboard cut-outs. I hated them on sight.

O reached into his shoulder holster and gave them his piece. I followed suit, and satisfied that we had been relieved of our weapons they opened the huge door to a darkened room. The first thing that hit me was the smell. The room reeked of human decay: of unwashed feet, rotting teeth and death – BQ's morgue smelled like a wedding party compared to the stench that filled the room. But before I could say anything O had already stepped forward into the gloom and there was nothing I could do but follow.

As the mercenaries closed the doors behind us, and the little light it had provided was snuffed out, darkness reclaimed the room. I heard shuffling feet and curtains being drawn, then more shuffling and more curtains opening until the room was filled with late-afternoon sunlight. Then, from the sudden blaze of light, a sickly, balding, Gandhi-like figure wrapped in a dirty white sheet emerged, poured some water into a beaten-up pot and placed it on the wood burner that sat incongruously in the middle of the dilapidated room. Now this is some weird shit, I thought. At last I could see what O had been trying to tell me earlier – Lord Thompson lived like an African, or more precisely he lived the stereotype of the African. The slave-master lived like a slave but in his mansion. He had converted his bedroom into slave quarters.

The water in the pot came to a boil almost immediately, and I watched as Lord Thompson threw in some tea leaves and sugar from two huge sacks next to the stove. A couple of minutes later he reached into a churn next to the wood burner and came out with a cup of milk that he added to the pot.

'Fresh from the farm,' he cried out to us as he stirred the pot a couple of times before lifting it from the fire and placing it on the dirty cement with his bare hands, flicking his fingers in the air to cool them down. 'Some tea, gentlemen?' he asked.

Lord Thompson poured his tea into two huge tin cups before producing a loaf of bread, which he promptly tore into three pieces using his bare hands – old, spotted and dirty. We had been standing all along, but once he had finished with his tea and bread, he waved us towards a number of three-legged stools arranged around the wood burner.

Once we had seated ourselves, and Lord Thompson had handed O and me our tea and bread, he sat down next to me, reached into his overalls and produced a pair of eyeglasses, to get a better look at me, he said.

'When I heard there was an American policeman on our

bit of the earth, I thought, why not invite him over?' Lord Thompson began. 'As my people say: He who does not leave his home thinks his mother is the best cook. I wanted you to taste my cooking before you return to your mother's.' His accent was very much like O's, but I could detect an English accent under the African one. 'I was expecting a white man,' he continued. 'But you, you surprise me.'

I hadn't thought that someone reading about me in the paper wouldn't be able to tell from my name that I wasn't white. I didn't ask him why it mattered – perhaps it was a calculated slight.

'And I must thank you for your hospitality,' I said as I tore into the bread and took a sip of tea. The tea was amazing! Who knew tea could taste like this? Fuck my coffee back in that dingy little café in Madison, I thought. I was moving on.

Lord Thompson surprised me because he wanted to know how the US economy was faring. He talked about the dollar in the world market and declared that the enemy of the United States was not Japan, which was buying America up, but China, which was buying up the treasury.

'So, Ishmael.' It took forever before the question left his mouth, but when it came it took me by surprise. 'Ishmael, where is your white whale? You have a white whale, don't you?' he asked in his half-African, half-British accent.

'I was named after my great, great-grandfather, Ishmael Fofona,' I replied coldly. 'I know who I am.'

'This Ishmael Fofona ... He must have been an African prince. You carry yourself rather well,' he said, seemingly genuinely unaware of the condescension in his words.

'And the white whale, it was Ahab not Ishmael ... '

I began, but then paused, realising that there was no point in antagonising the old man. We needed him more than he needed us. 'But, yes, I do have my own white whale ... ' I finished lamely.

'To kill or be killed by,' Lord Thompson said pointedly, looking at O. 'The devil will get us all in the end. Is that not so, O?'

'Just tell us why you called,' O said, putting a hard edge into his voice.

'Me and O here, we go way back,' Lord Thompson continued, ignoring O's question. 'Have you not told him? Come on now, Detective Odhiambo, that is not the way to treat your brother.' The amused contempt in the word brother was unmistakable.

O was silent.

'Ah, my dear brother ... ' Lord Thompson said, turning to me. 'So, he did not tell you, did he?' He paused as if gathering himself. 'Twice I have been acquitted,' he finally continued. 'One was self-defence. The other was purely accidental. I have the great fortune of African justice working in my favour, and O does not like it. Isn't that so, O?' he asked, still looking at me.

I turned to look at O, expecting some response, but he didn't say anything – he simply smiled, like he knew something Lord Thompson did not.

'O here thought I shot them like dogs,' the old man continued. 'But I was in front of a white judge and he acquitted me. That may not seem like much to you, but whites in this country hate me. Look around you. Whatever I am, I am African. My DNA is from my white parents, my skin is white, but my soul is African. I would never kill one of us,' he said with conviction.

O just kept smiling to himself.

'Enough of this,' Lord Thompson said, perhaps sensing that O wasn't going to give him the satisfaction of an argument. 'Ishmael, I will give you what you came for. Go to the Timbuktu Bar in Eastleigh. There you will find another guide. What you seek is in Africa. One dot connects the next. And as my people say: Only the traveller knows the road.' Having finished his speech he rang a little bell and the doors opened.

As I followed O out of Lord Thompson's room I wondered at the way I felt. I couldn't remember anyone eliciting so much anger and hatred from me in one meeting before. I wanted to hit him so bad, break a bone or two and force him to see the world he had created around him for what it really was – a lie. Perhaps it wasn't all about him? Perhaps it was about my relationship to white folk back in the US, but whatever it was it was powerful. And to claim that he was African? What the fuck was that all about? I was beginning to hate actively, I realised as O and I retrieved our weapons from the mercenaries, and I didn't like it. Facts and truth get lost in hate.

Making our way back to Eastleigh in the Land Rover, we talked about our next move and Lord Thompson's motives. This much we knew: the old man had more information than he had given us. But we also knew that we were finally on to something. There was nothing more we could do except play along until he had revealed his hand. We had to be cautious. Mistakes, hesitations, miscalculations – no more of that, we had to be at our best.

❰ We got to Timbuktu Bar around eight pm. I entered first. The place was empty save for the bartender and a butcher in a bloody apron – probably fresh from slaughtering what would soon become the evening's *nyama choma*. It wasn't an upscale place, but unlike The Hilton Hotel bar it did have a cement floor, an iron roof and jukebox. There was nothing to do except wait, so I asked for a Tusker and sat in a booth. O came in a few minutes later, sat at the counter farthest from the entrance and ordered a Tusker as well.

After a little while people started trickling into the bar and the jukebox came to life, blaring *Lingala* song after *Lingala* song – the music all sounded the same, with an annoyingly high-pitched guitar solo at the end of each song. By midnight the place was almost packed. It was an odd mixture of people – different races and classes. The well-to-do folk – some white, some black – were drinking liquor while the rest of us sipped our Tuskers. Couples slipped in and out of the bathroom. Sometimes money changed hands – for drugs or sex, I assumed.

Two hours later I was getting a little tipsy, and was at the point where I was thinking I should just join O at the counter and make a night of it – none of the people in the bar had looked in any way suspicious or sent a look of recognition my way. But just at that moment, a young couple started arguing loudly in Kiswahili by the jukebox, presumably over what to play. People looked on and laughed in amusement. Finally, the couple found a song, Bob Marley's 'Is This Love', a staple from my college days, and before long they were dancing and kissing to whistles and cheers from the tipsy crowd. O made eye contact to ask what I thought of them. I shook my head and he turned back to his beer.

Half an hour later, I was done with waiting, and decided to go to bathroom before joining O at the bar. Standing up, I finished what was left of my Tusker. I had long ago learned the hard way never to leave half of anything out in the open when working a case. Once, when I had just made detective, I was on a petty drugs case. Well, the fucker I was following slipped a heavy laxative in my coffee. Of course, I lost him and spent a whole day in the bathroom, burning ass and all. Finally, a uniform arrested him for drunk driving, but it had taken a long time to live it down.

I was thinking about that and how this thankless job is not without its humorous moments as I peed, half smiling to myself when the door opened. It was the young man from the jukebox. He nodded drunkenly. I continued taking my piss. Then, from the corner of my eye, I saw a blur of movement. I turned, pissing all over the place – on him and the walls – as I barely managed to stop him burying a knife in my neck.

When faced with a knife you will get injured, it's just a question of where and how badly. The main thing is to protect your wrists and vital organs. Everything else is fair game. Luckily the man was quite a bit shorter than me, and after his initial attack I managed to grab him in a way that meant he could only jab the knife ineffectually into my shoulder.

Unable to reach for my gun, I finally pushed the knife above us, stepped in and kneed him in the stomach. He doubled over, and holding his right hand up with my left I gave him an uppercut so that his head snapped backwards, then I brought his hand down behind his back so that he spun around. But even as the knife clattered to the floor I heard two gunshots above the music in the bar and the sound of screaming.

Seconds later the woman the young man had been dancing with walked in with what looked like a .32 in her hand. She had shot O. I was now alone.

I couldn't let the young man go. I had to use him as a shield while reaching for my gun. She yelled something to him in Kiswahili and he ducked down, moving to the left. I felt a bullet whizz just past my right shoulder. Then he suddenly leapt away from me, stumbling into the urinal, leaving me exposed. I threw myself to the ground as I went for my gun, but I already knew it was too late.

She's got the drop on me, I thought as I saw her narrow her eyes as she took aim. And, worse, my dick is hanging out of my pants. There was just time for the image of the dead white girl to flash through my mind one last time before the young woman's gun went off.

For a moment I thought I was hit, but it was just the shock of landing hard on the floor. I looked up at her in surprise as her gun clattered to the floor and she sank to the ground with a look of incomprehension on her face – a thin trickle of blood running down her dress and onto her legs. Then I saw O standing behind her, bracing himself against the bathroom wall, a smoking gun in his hand.

The man contemplated us – calculating his choices I suppose – but it was all over; he had played out his hand.

I stood up and zipped up my pants. 'Who sent you?' I asked the man.

'You, you *mzungu* tourist, we want money,' he screamed back, trying to wipe my piss and whatever else was in the urinal out of his eyes.

'Motherfucker, you call me a white man one more time and I'll shoot you right here,' I answered him. I was really tired of the *mzungu* shit.

O carefully unbuttoned his jacket and shirt. I could see two bullets lodged neatly in his vest, over his heart. 'She called my name, I turned and she shot me,' he said, grimacing in pain. Even with a vest, you still get quite a knock and he would be lucky if he hadn't broken a rib. He staggered over and stood over the young man, his gun trained on him.

'I tell you who sent me, you let me go,' the young man said. It was half a statement, half a question.

'Who sent you?' I asked him.

'Tell us what we want to know and you live,' O offered.

'I tell you, I go?' he asked with disbelief.

'To prison you dumb piece of shit,' I shouted at him.

'No deal ... ' He put his hand over his mouth to show he wasn't willing to talk.

'Pick her up!' O ordered him.

The young man hesitated and O shot at the wall just above his head.

'Pick her up and put her on your shoulder,' O shouted.

The young man scrambled to his feet, grabbed the dead woman by the waist and with some trouble hoisted her to his shoulder.

'You tell us what we want to know and we let you carry your dead. You are a soldier ... Tell us who gave the order,' O said gently, with the kind of patronising understanding that an officer might use when questioning an enemy soldier. I had never heard him speak like that before, but to my surprise it worked.

'Lord Thompson . . . ' the man said, his legs beginning to tremble with the effort of keeping the woman slung over his shoulder. 'We do works for him all the time. He call, we go to his place. He pay, we work.'

'Did he tell you why?' I asked him.

'No, no, no . . . He use code: "Cut weed from garden". He pay, we do. No questions,' he said, his eyes darting from my face to O's as he wondered which one of us had the power to let him go.

'You can go,' O finally said, holstering his gun.

❝ The man stumbled out of the bathroom and we followed – by now his back was covered in the woman's blood and he left a trail of it in his wake. The bar was empty. Only the bartender remained.

'Give me the money Lord Thompson paid you,' I said to the man.

He hesitated, looked at O and then with his free hand he reached into his pocket and took out a wad of notes. I walked to the bartender and gave him the money.

Outside, in the street, the crowd from the bar – white and black, rich and poor – had formed itself into an angry mob, and as we emerged they started spitting and yelling at the man. We stood for a while and watched as he tried to carry the body of the woman through the throng, but it wasn't long before they descended on him – punching and kicking. It was hard to believe this was the same crowd that was dancing just a few minutes ago. Finally, after what seemed like an eternity, he and the body he was carrying fell to the ground. Only then did O shoot several times into the air, and in the relative calm that followed tell the crowd to let the man go. By then the young man was sobbing, his legs trembling, but somehow he once again managed to pick up his accomplice, get her body over his shoulder and stagger off into the night.

We got into O's Land Rover as the crowd filed back into the bar – with us gone it was no longer a crime scene.

'Why did you let him go?' I asked O.

'If we'd taken him with us we'd have to babysit him,' he replied curtly. 'And anyway, you had already pissed all over him ... ' He laughed and started up the Land Rover.

Without asking, I knew we were going to pay Lord Thompson a visit. The old fuck had tried to kill us and now we needed to find out why. He was the link we had been looking for.

'All of this is just a game to him,' O explained as he turned back onto the main road. 'He could have had us back at the farm. It would have been easy enough. But, no, he has to send us on some wild goose chase to some bar ... '

I couldn't argue with that, it seemed to be well within the old man's character, so instead I asked O what his deal was with Lord Thompson. It was time for a fuller explanation.

'The first guy he killed was a poacher,' O started. 'Thompson hunted him. I mean he tracked him down like an animal and shot him. The Africans out on the farm told me. But in the end he was not even booked.' He paused. 'Poachers do not get much sympathy from me, but you don't kill a man for killing an animal, I don't care how beautiful it looks. Take him to prison, but do not kill him. The other guy he killed was a game warden. He was out on Thompson's property looking for poachers. Again Lord Thompson tracked him down and afterwards claimed that he mistook him for a poacher. But that's very unlikely. The guy was in a bright green game warden's uniform. But he got away with it again: white skin and wealth equals impunity.'

'Ain't that the truth everywhere,' I said to him.

'And there are other rumours I could never get to the bottom of: rapes and disappearances. That farm is his kingdom,' O said.

I was suddenly very curious. O had told me that he had become a cop because he didn't make it into the one and only university in Kenya, but in light of what I had seen of him his answer seemed flippant. What had made him so irresolute in his definition of good and evil? And where did his screwed-up sense of crime and punishment come from? I asked him, and well, he had a story to match my Random Killer story.

'Well, let's see ... ? A few years back a rich guy, his wife and two young children were murdered. Shot. With the rich shits it is almost always about money and rarely about sex. So, we followed the money and it led us straight to his business partner. Amos Kamau, that is the partner's name, wanted to make all the money. It was not like their car import business was going bankrupt. It was not even a criminal enterprise, where the rules of the jungle might apply. They were a legit car import company that was doing well, making them both rich, but Amos just wanted everything for himself. So, we arrested him, but within a week we were ordered to release him, and just like that he was out. Everyone now knew he was a killer, no doubt, but he was out, bribed his way out. He wanted to make a point, so he asked that I drive him home. On the way I asked him whether he really did it. And he said yes. Why, I asked him. Guess what the little shit said? "Because I could get away with it." Today he is chairing fund-raisers for politicians, giving money to poor children and generally living it up. His crime has been forgotten because of his good deeds.

'A few weeks later, a poor man found a thousand shillings, just like that. He went home, fetched his wife and two kids and took them for *nyama choma* and ice cream. They had a good time. But when they got home, he killed them all. The neighbours called us. We got there to find him sitting outside his hut, his panga still wet with blood. No resistance from him. As I drove him to the station I asked him why he did it. He said he had been working all his life, waiting for a break. After thirty years, his only lucky break had been the thousand shillings. He had killed his family to spare them the hardships of the kind of life he was able to provide for them. So, I told him that his story would make sense only if he had killed himself as well, or at least tried to kill himself, but with him alive it looked like plain murder. I turned to look at him and he leaned closer and said: "But I am not mad." It was not denial; his actions were those of a sane man who had come to the end of his road … He was hanged soon after,' O said. 'And the rich guy? What does he get in the end? Everything.

'So, after that I started believing in justice I could see. We live in anarchy; life is cheap and the rich and the criminals can buy a whole lot of it. Meantime, someone has to be on the side of justice. Janet … That young man would have been out of jail the following day for five hundred shillings, and he would have found her. Maybe what I do matters, maybe it doesn't, I don't know.' O stopped as if suddenly feeling self-conscious as his musings became scattered. 'Ah, O the philosopher, the modern Socrates,' he added with a laugh.

His story made sense and it didn't, just like my Random Killer story – at some point it broke down. But intuitively it made sense. Or perhaps we all have an ink-blot case – the case that we use to justify every fucked-up thing we do.

'Well, let's go arrest the fucker,' I said to O. 'He can't get away with it this time.'

❝ At the gate we found two black guards warming themselves by a fire. It was two thirty am. O rolled his window down and showed them his badge, then he got out of the car. He spoke to them in Kiswahili for a few minutes, to explain the situation, I gathered. The guards didn't say anything. They simply lifted the gate and we drove in. It didn't surprise me – Lord Thompson wasn't worth their lives, and rather than engage us it was simply easier to let us through. Thompson's whiteness had long been a shield only because the black people around him held it up. And in return? Humiliation and murder were his stock-in-trades. It could have been revenge for the murders, or for his owning so much land while they owned nothing, or for mocking them by imitating what he thought the essence of African life to be, but the end result was the same – our being allowed into the house without as much as a single alarm going off.

This time we did not have to ring the bell – the guards had called ahead to their colleagues by the big oak doors and they stood open. When we got to Thompson's bedroom, his two mercenaries were standing by the doors smoking. They hadn't been informed of our arrival and we shot them as they fumbled for their AK-47s. They didn't stand a chance.

As we made sure the mercenaries were really dead we heard screaming coming from inside Lord Thompson's room. O threw open the bedroom door, but the gunshots must have registered as part of a nightmare, because although the old man was tossing and turning in his bed when we walked in, he was quite obviously fast asleep.

We turned the lights on, then woke him up. It took him a moment to adjust to the light before he yelled for his mercenaries. We waited for him to realise they weren't coming to his rescue.

'They are dead. It's just you, O and me,' I explained.

Dressed in his striped pyjamas, in his mahogany bed surrounded by squalor he looked truly comical.

'Njoroge!' he yelled for his help.

A few seconds later Njoroge sauntered in. He looked over at us and at the old man. 'Sir, what seems to be the problem?' he asked, but Lord Thompson didn't understand him, he just looked at us with confusion.

'Sir, everything seems to be in order,' Njoroge continued calmly. 'Have a good night.' And with that he closed the door behind him. It was as if he had been practising those exact words his entire life.

Terror registered on the old man's face. Betrayed by his black help, the nightmare that his whiteness had protected him from was standing before him.

'You know why we are here?' I asked him.

'They failed, they failed, they failed,' he chanted as if he needed to hear himself say it before he knew it was true.

'Was it Joshua who asked you to do this?' I asked.

'I don't know. It was a white man. He asked me to help ... said it was important,' he answered.

'And will you kindly tell us who this white man is?' O asked as if Lord Thompson was a little kid.

'His name is Samuel Alexander. He works for ... '

'The Refugee Centre,' I said, interrupting him. 'And why did he ask you to have us killed?'

'I do not know. Samuel said that you and O were trying to bring him down. I did not ask anything more.'

It didn't make any sense. The old man was wealthy and protected and no one was forcing him to help Samuel.

'Why did you do it?' I couldn't stop myself from asking.

'I don't know, Ishmael. I don't know ... Because he asked,' he answered. 'Who knows why we really do anything.'

The poor fool, he couldn't see it. He had done it to preserve an old order of race and class – because a fellow white man had asked him. And because he could. The same reason why he had killed before.

'Listen, you are of no concern to me,' I said. From the corner of my eye I could see O was getting impatient. 'Give me something useful. What do you know about Joshua or the girl?'

'Nothing about your girl. But I have heard things about Joshua ... '

'What things?'

'That he can be cruel ... In public he is all smiles, but he has a mean streak, yelling and threatening people when he does not get his way,' the old man answered despairingly, only too aware of how useless his information was.

'You really don't know anything else, do you?' O asked the old man.

'The Refugee Centre, it's run by the Never Again Foundation,' Lord Thompson stammered. 'To get to the truth, get to the Never Again Foundation.'

'That we know. Try again, old man,' I said, hoping he had more information – something conclusive – even though I knew he did not.

'I told you this day would come,' O said to him almost absent-mindedly.

'I have lived for a long time,' the old man replied, 'but if you are going to kill me, at least let me die with some dignity.'

O didn't say anything, so the old man looked at me, but I averted my eyes.

'Let me die like a man!' he shouted.

I was torn. I wanted to stop O, but Lord Thompson had two murders to answer for, and if things had gone his way, we would have been dead as well.

Walking over to a large chest, Lord Thompson removed a leopard skin, a beaded whisk and a large, regal-looking hat made out of lion-hide. Then, taking off his pyjamas, he put on his African best – finishing the effect by tying a number of brightly coloured amulets around his ankles. Finally, he stood up straight, and took a deep breath as if preparing for his death, but at the last minute his courage failed him.

'Listen, Ishmael, I might know something ... ' he said. 'Okay? Okay? Let me think.' He didn't even pause. 'Some African wisdom for you, eh, Ishmael?' He gestured to me as one would to a person with whom one had something in common – as if we had some secret partnership that excluded O. 'To catch ants, you use honey. You use honey to catch ants, you use cunning to …'

He didn't finish the sentence because O shot him once through the head. Then, taking a lighter from his pocket, he struck a flame and threw it onto the bed which soon caught fire. There was a fury and logic in him I was beginning to understand – maybe because I was becoming like him. O had drawn a line between what he considered his world and the outside world. The good people – his wife, Janet, the dead white girl – existed in the outside world. When he was in that world, he was visiting and he behaved accordingly. He did not carry his bad dreams and conscience into it. But sometimes those from his world went to the outside world and did terrible things. And when he came across them, or they crossed back into his world, there were no rules, and there was no law. There was a duality to him that was so complete that he moved between the two worlds seamlessly.

'Come on, Ishmael, we have to go,' O said gently as smoke started to fill the room. 'He was supposed to have died a long time ago.'

But even as O turned to leave I fell to my knees and threw up. Having narrowly escaped being killed twice in the three short days I had been in Nairobi, I had wondered whether I was becoming blasé about the taking of a human life, but obviously a little piece of my conscience was still alive and well in this fucked-up place. I understood that in O's world justice was long overdue, but that didn't stop me from pitying the old man – there was something pitiable in him and perhaps, for

72

that reason alone, we should have let him live.

❝ We heard a loud explosion as we finally made our way out of Lord Thompson's room, and following the noise we soon found ourselves in what turned out to be a massive sitting room. The Africans who worked for Thompson had, using God knows what, blown up the wall safe and dollar bills and pound notes were floating in the air. I understood. They had to get what they could that night. Sure, the old white man was dead, but it wouldn't be long before some rich African bastard ended up with the farm, and then they would be right back where they started. It was the way of the world everywhere.

'Let us pay Samuel Alexander a visit,' O said as we made our way out of Lord Thompson's mansion.

I watched the fire spread through the house as O called the station on the Land Rover's radio. A few minutes later someone called back with an address.

'What if the old man had more for us?' I finally asked.

'He didn't,' O said confidently.

'How the fuck do you know?'

'People like him have no loyalties ... they protect nothing ... would not die for anything. If he had something more, he would have spilled his guts,' O reasoned calmly, ignoring my tone. 'And, anyway, we got what we came for. We are making progress, no?' he asked sounding a little like Joshua.

I felt too exhausted to question his logic or interrogate what he was calling progress.

'Ishmael, we are bad people too,' O said as he started the

Land Rover. 'The only difference is that we fight on the side of the good. I hope you have no illusions about that.'

« Samuel Alexander, no surprises, lived in Muthaiga. We went through several heavily fortified gates before we got to his house, which itself was surrounded by a high wall topped with razor wire and broken glass. 'This place is like a prison,' I said to O as we rang the doorbell.

Seeing a flicker behind the peephole, O showed his badge, explaining we were on urgent police business and we wanted to ask the boss a few routine questions. The man behind the door then asked that we slip both our badges under the door, which we did. Finally, he opened up – revealing himself to be an elderly African with a dignified face – and invited us into the house. He led us to the sitting room and told us to wait there while he ascertained whether Samuel was home.

The man returned to say that his boss wasn't answering his knock. Did he check the bedroom? He said no, he had just knocked. Was he sure Samuel Alexander was in? No, he wasn't sure, sometimes he came home late. He started to protest as we made our way to the first floor, but O just pushed him aside.

O knocked on what we guessed to be the bedroom. There was no answer. He tried the door and it opened. The bed was empty.

O drew his weapon and I did the same. The housekeeper, who had followed us up, backed away and went quickly back down the stairs as we walked through the bedroom to the bathroom. I knocked on the bathroom door, but once again there was no answer. I opened the door. Samuel Alexander was in the bathtub, neck-deep in bloody water, his hands with slit wrists floating in the water.

We didn't have to look far for the note. It had been prominently placed on the bathroom sink. It was addressed to Joshua. It said: *I AM SORRY*. Nothing more. Sorry for what? Did Samuel Alexander have something to do with the white girl? Was he involved in setting Joshua up? If so, why? And, if not, then what was the connection?

We searched the house, looking for anything that might help, but there was nothing that obviously tied Samuel Alexander to Joshua. Not even the housekeeper knew anything of use. Once again we had come to a dead end.

Half an hour later we watched aimlessly as a Kenyan paramedic unplugged the tub so that he and his colleague could lift the body out. As the water drained, we made out a locket – he must have been holding it in his hand. The paramedic handed it to me, and I walked over to the sink where I opened it. Bloody water ran out, but to my pleasant surprise the twin photographs behind the glass were not wet. I dabbed the locket dry. On the left there was small photograph of Samuel. On the right there was black-and-white photograph of a black woman with long curly hair. In the photo she was smiling as if someone had just said something to her. She was beautiful.

'Only an unspeakable thing would make a man commit suicide when he has a woman like her,' O pronounced over my shoulder, and I nodded in agreement.

One more piece to fit somewhere in the puzzle ...

We walked out of the bedroom behind the paramedics and watched as they manhandled the body down the stairs and out to the ambulance. In the sitting room we found Samuel Alexander's housekeeper sitting in an armchair crying into a white apron. I tapped him on the shoulder and showed him the photograph. He stared at the woman. 'It was her. He did it for her,' he said, pointing a shaking finger at her.

'Who is she?' I asked.

He didn't know, only that he had not seen her around for a while now – a year or so. She and Samuel Alexander were lovers – she had slept over many times. And he didn't know her name? Master – at last that word came out of his mouth – never told him anything. They walked in late at night, and left early in the morning.

'Look here, old man, your master was not here to stay,' O said to the housekeeper sarcastically. 'He would have gone back to his country. What difference does it make to your sorry ass how he departs?'

The old man looked at O. Even I was shocked at his callousness. 'You are a cruel man, young man. Someday the sky will fall on you,' the old man replied and spat on the clean floor.

'Take what you can and go home to your grandchildren,' O said, his voice emotionless.

The bodies were piling up fast, I thought as we made our way outside. And I had the feeling that I would soon find myself on the top of the heap unless something gave.

'If they came home late, it must have been from the bars ... ' O said as we climbed into the Land Rover. 'Tomorrow we'll hit as many as we can. With her looks we will find her sooner or later.'

" When we got home around five we found Maria still up, she had curled herself up in the dining room, dressed in nothing but a sleeping gown, and was reading and sipping hot chocolate. She wasn't raving mad like my ex – throwing a fit and threatening divorce. Instead she was reading a fun novel – 'putting in a little me time' before she went to work. O kissed her and went to take a shower, but I hung around.

'Don't you ever worry about O?' I asked her when he was out of earshot.

'Yes, I do worry,' she said with feeling, 'but we are what we do and you cannot take a human being in parts. Marriage doesn't work like that. You take the good and the bad and hope for the best.'

'I wish my ex was as philosophical,' I said to her as I made a move towards the spare bedroom.

'Philosophy has nothing to do with it,' she said with a laugh. 'We don't ask for those that we love. Maybe I am just resigned to my lot?' She paused. 'And just so as you know, you are bleeding all over my floor.'

I had no idea what she was talking about.

She pointed to my shoulder. 'If it is not as bad as it looks, there is an emergency kit in the bathroom cabinet,' she said and took a sip of her hot chocolate.

I couldn't understand what was going on. Maria didn't even pretend to want to know what had happened to my shoulder, or why I stank horribly. And O hadn't explained. The American in me wanted to call it denial – but if it worked for them, it worked.

O was leaving the bathroom as I walked in. I took a shower and washed the stab wounds with Dettol. They stung harshly but they weren't deep. Having cleaned my wounds I bandaged my shoulder, found a cleaning cloth in the bathroom and went to the sitting room to wipe up the blood.

Having cleaned up after myself I said goodnight to O and his wife, who were sitting on the couch, looking every bit the normal couple, and went to bed. Before I could fall asleep, they started making love. I sat there listening to them, thinking about the life my parents had mapped out for me. I missed it. I suppose we all miss some other kind of life, a parallel life.

Finally, O and Maria left the sitting room and went to their bedroom. For a while all I could hear was the murmur of their voices, followed every now and then by laughter, and it was to this sound that I drifted off to sleep.

I WOULD RATHER DRINK MUDDY WATERS

❝ *I was sitting at my desk. Mo walked in naked, in high heels, but the other cops went about their business as if she wasn't there. She came to me and unzipped my pants. As my penis slid into her, she took my gun and placed it on my forehead. Suddenly she had a huge basket of vanilla ice cream. With her bare hand, she started feeding it to me in bigger and bigger quantities until I felt like I was drowning. My stomach was getting bigger and bigger and my penis smaller and smaller until it slid out of her. And just when my stomach was about to burst from too much ice cream I woke up, belching and looking for my dick. I couldn't help laughing. Who has a wet dream that is also a nightmare?*

I looked at the time – it was two in the afternoon. I dressed quickly and went to find O. He was in a cloud of smoke in the kitchen, smiling contentedly. This wasn't the same man I had been with the day before and as I stared at his smiling face I realised that I was also in a better mood, in spite of everything – I was well rested, had made a little bit of progress, and had an assurance that I was looking in the right places.

'Listen, you schizoid sonofabitch,' I said to O half

playfully, half annoyed that we had wasted a whole morning, 'we have work to do.'

'Yes, we do,' he said, 'but bars around here don't open till four.'

He had a point. The woman in the photograph was our only lead and if she worked in a bar it made more sense to go looking for her in the evening.

O made his omelette for me and incredibly the masterpiece seemed to taste even better the third time around. 'It needed a little less onion and a little more coriander,' he explained as we were eating. Then he contemplated me for a while. Finally, he said, 'Tell me, how does it feel to be black in your country? Tell me how it really feels … '

'Don't you ever just smoke in peace?' I said, raising my hands up into the air.

'I am a philosopher by nature, you know,' O replied. 'So, tell me.'

'Look, O, I can't say I know. How does it feel? When I am by myself I don't feel black. I mean, how do you define yourself? What would you say you are?'

'A Luo,' O answered.

'So, are you a Luo when you are by yourself or only when you are with non-Luos?' I asked him.

'But there are things that I do when I am by myself that only a Luo would do,' he replied.

'But do you wake up, look at yourself in the mirror, and say to yourself that the Luo looks tired this morning? I mean, I don't go to bed black or wake up black. I don't look at myself in the mirror and say I am black. Black is what white folk see. You'd better ask them.'

'What do you think they would say?' O asked, unwilling to give up his line of questioning.

'How the fuck am I supposed to know, do I look white to you?'

'Shit, man, take it easy, man. I just wanted to know,' he said defensively. 'Allow me, kind sir, to ask you another one.'

'Go ahead, but it had better not be a question I can't answer.'

'How do you feel being here? I mean, here in Kenya ... as a black man from America?'

Now that was a tough question.

'Look, man, I like to keep it simple,' I began. 'I like you, but I like your wife better. I like the food and the beer, but I detest Mathare and whatever it is that keeps people there. I hate your city, with its skyscrapers that are trying to reach the white man's kingdom, and I sure as hell hate your justice system. How do I feel? I want to find my killer and bring him to justice ... that's all.'

O kept quiet for a while. 'I like your answer,' he finally said and broke into laughter. 'Very, very philosophical.'

❮ After brunch, O and I got ready to hit the town. Hoping not to attract attention, O was wearing a suit jacket, a black polo neck, brown pants and brown dress shoes. In the US he might have stood out, but in Nairobi he blended in with the middle class seamlessly. I, on the other hand, was dressed in a black suit and a white T-shirt, and though I was sure I would still stand out I didn't feel as excessively American as I had a few days earlier. Perhaps, I thought, it had all been in my head.

As we walked towards the Land Rover O threw the keys to me. 'You drive,' he said. 'I think this time I am too high, for real.'

In the US everyone complains about the traffic in New York, but in Nairobi it's anarchy. There was only one thing to do and that was to use the siren. With it blaring O directed me around traffic circles and down one-way streets until we made it to the city centre.

Once there we had a decision to make. Did we look for the girl in high-, middle-, or low-class joints? Judging from her photograph and what we knew about Samuel Alexander, a well-to-do expatriate, we figured they either patronised really high-class places or the kind of dives that would have given them an 'authentic' African experience. There was nothing in-between about the woman – either Samuel Alexander had found her as she was or he had picked her up in the gutter somewhere and cleaned her up. We decided to start with the hole in the walls – we could scare people into talking more easily there than in the upper-class joints.

We took a matatu to the bottom end of River Road – from here we would work our way upwards. 'River Road is a dangerous part of town. This was where the famous Mr Henderson was gunned down,' O narrated as we climbed out of the matatu.

O told me that Henderson had been a British colonial officer who had become head of the CID after independence. He was so mean that even the most hardened criminals feared him. A giant of a man, he was the only cop who could walk alone in River Road and no one would as much as look him in the eye. Well, what had worked well in colonial times didn't work so well after twenty years of independence. 'By then even the criminals were nationalists,' O said with a laugh. 'They wanted to be hunted down by black cops.'

So, a notorious bank robber by the name of Koitalel followed Henderson to River Road, called him by his name, so that he turned around, and shot him twice in the chest with a shotgun. 'For good measure,' O said.

But Henderson didn't die right away, so Koitalel went over and introduced himself, and Henderson, ever the soldier, begged that he finish him off quick. Koitalel obliged, using Henderson's colonial-era pistol. Everyone in River Road saw it happen, but no one dared to call the police, giving Koitalel plenty of time to make his escape. By the time the police were informed of what had happened Koitalel was nowhere to be found, and somehow, despite a protracted manhunt, he managed to slip through the net. Nobody knows what became of him, though some say he went for plastic surgery and became a politician – a rumour that O told me had at one time been banned. 'My theory is that he was one of those thugs disciplined enough to stop after he had made enough,' O said. 'He's probably somewhere in Uganda even as we speak.'

'You sound like you admired the fucker,' I said when he was done.

'I hated Henderson. But I would have given anything to be the one to hunt Koitalel down. Those were the days when cops and thugs made each other heroes. Now it's mostly just idiots: car thieves and rapists,' he answered. 'But your Joshua, he might turn out to be one of the great ones, better even than your Random Killer.'

We were now at Government Road and there was just one bar left. Someone had parked a new bright green BMW outside, but the joint itself was a dingy little place with Camel Lights posters plastered all over the place and a pool table without any felt. We sat at the counter and waited for the bartender to come over. When he finally acknowledged us O showed him the photograph, and he pointed to the corner of the counter. 'Talk to the bossman, I have not been here a very long time,' he said in heavily accented English.

By then my eyes had adjusted to the darkness enough to make out the massive man sitting at the corner of the bar. Dressed in a green suit, he was reading the paper and sipping occasionally at a glass of water. That explains the green BMW outside, I thought to myself. He obviously liked to match his car.

Leaving O at the counter I walked over to the man, greeted him and showed him the photograph. He looked at it, then at me and finally went back to reading his paper.

'Ever seen her around?' I asked him.

'What do you think?' he growled.

'Just trying to find her,' I explained, trying to keep my cool.

'No, never seen her,' he answered.

I thanked him and started walking away. 'Hey, listen … Don't be hasty. Information here is not free,' he called out after me.

'How much?' I asked, reaching for my wallet and taking out two thousand Kenyan shillings.

He pulled back as if I was trying to hand him a dirty rag. 'American dollars! You are a rich *mzungu*, a rich man like you …'

I didn't let him finish the sentence – I was very tired of the *mzungu* shit, it was liked being called a nigger over and over again, and the word nigger is always a fighting word. I hit him hard in the face and followed with a left jab to his throat. Then I picked up his glass of water and smashed it over his head, pushing him off his stool, which I picked up and broke over his back. With big fat men, I've learned my lesson: don't fight fair and always draw first blood, it takes the fight out of them. Well, sometimes, because instead of going down and staying down this man roared in anger, and getting to his feet he lifted me up into the air and slammed me against the wall. He pulled back for a body slam, but I sidestepped and punched him twice in the stomach, then as he reached out to get a hold of me, I poked him hard in the eyes. Then, as he bellowed in pain, I hit him with a hard right cross, the blow that finally put him down.

I looked over at O. He was looking at the bartender with a slight smile on his face, but the bartender had obviously decided that his job description didn't include leaping to his boss's defence. O swivelled around on his bar stool, turning his attention to the fat man and me. I pointed to the two thousand shillings on the floor, and O slid off his bar stool and picked them up. Then, pulling himself back to his feet, he put the money down on the counter. 'Take this and get lost,' he said to the bartender.

The bartender looked confused.

'How much do you make in a month?' O asked, pressing the bloody notes into the man's hands.

'About seven thousand,' the bartender answered.

'Well then, go on, open the till and tell me how much is there,' O said lazily.

The bartender jerked it open and counted out about three thousand shillings in notes.

'That makes five thousand. Fat man, what have you got in your wallet?' O asked him.

He had six thousand, which O also handed over to the bartender.

'And take some liquor with you,' O told him. 'The expensive shit.'

The fat man groaned as the bartender retrieved a bottle of Jameson and one of Chivas Regal from the display case above the bar.

When the bartender finally left, we locked the door behind him and helped the fat man to his feet and onto one of the bar stools. Then O went behind the counter, found a bottle of Jack Daniel's and served each of us a shot.

'We need to talk,' he said, placing the bottle on the counter. 'Drink that.'

The fat man downed the shot and O poured him another.

'The girl in the photo ... ' the fat man started to say.

'No, no, no, wait, don't you have something to say to my friend first?'

'I am sorry.'

'Sorry for what?' O asked him.

'Sorry for calling you a white man,' the fat man said, looking down into his glass of whiskey.

'Very well, continue ... ' O said.

'The girl in the photo, yes, I know her. She used to work here ... Fucking ungrateful refugees. She was beautiful, brought in a lot of customers.' He picked a bar rag off the counter and tried to clean some of his blood off his suit. 'Then, one day, this white man came in. I don't know what they talked about, but she just took off her apron and left with him. Next thing I know she is a big thing over at Club 680.'

'What is her name?' I asked.

'We called her Madeline. Can't say if it was real or not. With refugees, you never know.'

'Have you ever seen this man?' I showed him Joshua's photograph.

He looked at it for a while. 'Everyone knows Joshua, but that was years ago. A hero, but we did not know it then, nobody knew until much later. He was quiet, only spoke to Madeline ... '

'Were they fucking?'

'I don't know. She was a strange girl ... '

The connections, very hazy still, were slowly coming to the surface. Samuel had placed Joshua in Kenya for me, but he had told us that their meetings had been purely business related. Now I had placed both Samuel and Joshua here, in this bar, and I had a lead on someone who might have known him well – someone who certainly knew Samuel Alexander well. I still had no idea who the white girl was. To find that out, I first had to find out who Joshua really was, and to do that I had to find Madeline and learn more about Samuel.

'Is that you?' O suddenly asked in disbelief. He was pointing at a photograph of a boxer hitting a punching bag, youth and muscles still glowing down at us from up on the wall.

'I used to be a boxer,' the fat man said out of nowhere,

without looking up from his whiskey. 'I used to be really good.'

'Yes, yes, I remember you now,' O said with genuine excitement, 'you knocked out Peter "Dynamite" Odhiambo. What the hell happened to you?'

'*Nyama choma* and beer,' the fat man replied as if he was reminiscing with old friends. 'Back then I could have taken both of you ... easy.'

'Even the best lose eventually,' I offered, suddenly feeling sorry for him – for what we had done to him in such a short time, for breaking him so easily. 'Besides, I did not fight fair.'

'Yeah, is not that the truth,' the fat man said. 'Tomorrow it might be you.' He laughed before grimacing in pain.

Our conversation over, we left him there – bleeding into his counter, drinking straight from the bottle – and made our way to Club 680.

❦ There was no mistaking Madeline. She was up on a small stage, behind her a dreadlocked guitarist. People were clapping wildly. She waved them quiet as we took our seats at the bar, then turned so as to face the back of the stage. 'Enough with the political shit,' she whispered into the microphone.

I thought she was introducing a song, but before long I realised that this was a spoken word performance.

Silence descended as the guitarist took off his wedding ring and replaced it with a glass guitar slide. He tested the sound, so that for a moment the whole bar, dimly lit save for the stage, was filled with a bluesy sound. And then, starting to speak in slow rap, she joined the guitarist: 'My hair has roots all over the earth, like the roots of an old, old, old baobab, tapping and traversing the whole earth.'

Turning sideways, she leaned back as she undid the wrap around her head so that long thin dreadlocks unfurled, almost touching the ground, completing her arc.

'And my skin, this old raggedy skin thing … ' The crowd laughed and even I smiled because her dark skin, glistening from oil or sweat or both, was so smooth that it looked soft to the touch and anything but ragged.

'This old skin is the same skin my great-grandmother wore to sleep and to the garden, this is the skin that she wore when in battle. Don't be fooled by its softness, in peace it's for pleasure, but it quickly grows scales when it's time for war.' She caressed the length of first one arm and then the other, back and forth, back and forth until her skin seemed to radiate her blackness. Then, as she raised her hands up high with her fists clenched, the guitarist hit some violent chords, making his instrument sound like machine-gun fire and missiles.

'And these breasts, these breasts can feed a child and bring a grown man to tears in the same evening.' The crowd laughed approvingly – she was tall, about my height, and slender, but when she thrust her chest forward the T-shirt she wore to her midriff hugged her breasts tightly.

'And my hands, they are rough from play and lifting machetes. They can undress you, or they can peel my covers away.' She lifted her T-shirt up until we could see the beginning of her breasts.

'And my mouth can curse or love, speak hope or pain, but when you are good to me, let's just say my tongue wraps around things easily.' She raised her hands high in the air and ground her hips.

'And this, this is not a treasure to be beheld from afar, when you come closer, when you come closer you will see that it will lead your tongue to my pleasure.' Her hand followed the small chain that hung from a sparkling belly button ring down into her jeans. And then she broke into an easy laughter as if to remind the audience it was a performance after all.

'What the hell!' I heard O exclaim as the lights came up and everyone stood to give Madeline a standing ovation. It was an odd mixture of people, now that I could see them – elite Kenyans, refugees and expatriates. It reminded me of the mixture of people we had encountered in Mathare, only this was the other end of the scale.

After bowing first to the guitarist and then to the crowd Madeline made her way to the bar where men and their wives clamoured to shake her hand and buy her drinks. A few minutes later she was rescued from her fans by a gentleman who led her away to a table near the stage. O and I ordered drinks and kept watch, waiting for an opening, but it wasn't until an hour or so later that she stood up and walked to the bathroom. When she re-emerged I stood to intercept her, but instead of heading back to her table she came over to the bar.

'You are that detective? The American?' she asked after I had introduced myself and told her that we'd like to ask her a few questions. 'You want to know about Joshua?'

She did not betray any emotion beyond curiosity. I on the other hand was perspiring like an acne-ridden teenager out on a mercy date. Finally, having untied my tongue, I confirmed her suspicions but added there was another matter we also needed to talk about.

'Can it wait?' she asked.

And somehow, in the face of her request, the urgency of the whole case receded into the background. 'Yes, of course, I can wait,' I stammered.

Her drink came and, still looking at us, she leaned over the bar and whispered something to the bartender. Then she leaned in further over the counter and kissed him lightly on the cheek. 'Call me Muddy, it's short for Madeline,' she called over her shoulder to me as she turned away and walked back to her table.

'On her fans, gentlemen. They buy her more than she can drink,' the bartender explained a few minutes later as he placed six Tuskers in front of us.

'Now, that is what I like to hear,' O said.

A few minutes later the guitarist came and joined us. He was very young, in his early twenties, and still had the swagger and bravado of youth. He sat next to me and took one of the beers without saying anything. 'Muddy said I could,' he explained when I looked at him.

I had to laugh. We were like three little pigs at the trough – and her feeding us.

'You can jam, man. How long have you been playing for her?' I asked the guitarist after he had taken a long pull on the Tusker he had liberated.

'One year. She is good to me. You know? I came here from Rwanda, but I was very young. She is good to me . . . ' he said reflectively.

'You married?' O asked, pointing at his ring.

'No, this just for show . . . Makes it look serious when I take it off and put on the slide; replacing the wife with the guitar. That kinda symbolism works great for the crowd,' he said with a sly smile.

'Ever seen her with this man?' I asked, showing him the photo of Samuel Alexander that had been in the locket.

He laughed. 'She does not go with white men.'

'Perhaps you don't know her that well,' O said.

In the photograph in the locket her hair had been long and curly – her dreadlocks must have taken some time to grow.

'Have you ever met B.B. King?' the guitarist suddenly asked enthusiastically, changing the subject.

He looked disappointed when I told him I hadn't. 'But I saw Michael Jackson in concert once,' I added.

He shrugged. Michael no longer had the currency he used to.

We sat around without talking much. The bartender kept our trough full of beer, and O and the guitarist became visibly drunk. At some point I asked the guitarist why everyone called her Muddy, but he said he did not know. 'Could be something to do with Muddy Waters,' he said a minute or so later and started to hum 'Catfish Blues'. I joined him and before long we were all wailing away, out of tune, especially O, who didn't even know the song but sang anyway.

If you had told me a mere two weeks earlier that I would soon find myself in a bar in Africa singing 'Catfish Blues' with a schizoid detective called O and a blues guitarist from Rwanda, waiting on one of the most beautiful women I had ever seen, I would have told you straight out that you were crazy, but here I was.

Eventually, the bartender signalled to Muddy that he was closing up and she left her table and walked over to where we

92

were still drinking. 'If you want to talk you have to drive me home,' she said.

O handed me the keys to the Land Rover. As he did so, the guitarist stood up to come with us, but Muddy told him to stay with O and make sure he got home all right. She didn't have a purse or anything. I suppose she was all she needed. And before long, my date and I were on our way to her place.

❰ Muddy lived out in Limuru, thirty minutes or so outside of Nairobi, and as I drove her slender hand would, every now and then, point in this direction or that, guiding me first out of the city and then deep into the countryside. I was ready for whatever was ahead of me. Or more precisely, I didn't care what was ahead of me. My heart was beating fast; my mind full of stupid questions to ask her: 'Where are you from?', 'What music do you listen to?', 'What do your parents do?', 'What are your favourite colours?'. But in reality I knew that the get-to-know-you-questions from my teenage years wouldn't work, and as we drove deeper into the night I began to realise just how little actual dating I had really done.

Muddy punched in the knobs on the old radio and found a station that was playing country music. There aren't many things in this life that are certain, but that's one of them – a country music station anywhere in the world. Strangely, I didn't mind.

'Muddy … why do they call you Muddy?' I asked her.

Nobody wears safety belts in Africa, and she had her feet up on the dashboard, leaning towards me and humming along to Kenny Rogers as he sang a duet about not falling in love with dreamers.

'They call me Muddy, because the men I know would rather drink muddy waters,' she finally answered with a sigh, signalling with her hand that we should make a left off the main road onto a gravel track.

'What do you mean?' I asked her as the Land Rover's wheels hit the dirt road, creating a monotonous grinding noise that jarred heavily against the calm of country music – I'm not much of a blues man but drinking muddy waters didn't sound pleasant.

Instead of answering she asked me to slow down as we were approaching her gate, which a watchman opened as soon as she leaned her head outside the car window. She pulled a crumpled pack of cigarettes from her pocket and threw it at him as we crawled past.

Does everybody in this country live like a prisoner? I wondered as two huge Alsatian guard dogs came careering around the corner of the small house that now stood in front of us, barking furiously. It was as if the wealthy, the middle class, the farmers, the poor and even the criminals were all imprisoned in their own little worlds.

Climbing down from the Land Rover, Muddy calmed the dogs down before sending them back to the watchman. When he had them under control I opened my door and stepped out into her yard, watching as she unlocked security door after security door until finally we were inside her place and she turned on the lights.

The first thing that struck me was how simple everything was. The wooden furniture was spaced out in the sitting room so that it looked more like a low-class barroom. But she'd made it work, brightening the room up with paintings of little stick figures and wooden carvings. Her place reminded me of Joshua's in a strange way – even though, unlike Joshua's, it was clear that she lived there.

Muddy invited me into the kitchen – again very spare – and opened a cabinet that contained several bottles of expensive liquor. 'You know moonshine?' she asked me.

I nodded.

'Try this,' she said, reaching behind the glass bottles and producing a plastic container, 'it's African moonshine.'

She poured me a shot of clear liquid, and I grabbed it, ready to down it. 'You'd better sip it,' she advised, and as soon as it touched my tongue I knew why – it was almost pure alcohol.

'What is it called?' I asked her.

'*Changaa*,' she said.

Then, leaving me to my thoughts, Muddy went to change. She returned from the bathroom in what looked to me a like a dress-sized dashiki. Her dreads were down, so that when she sat at the kitchen counter, one hand cupped under her chin and the other shifting her shot glass back and forth, they dangled in front of her. She looked up at me – her eyes burrowing into mine – and I looked down at my hands. Cupping the shot glass they looked huge, and suddenly I felt like I was back at the airport all over again – all too aware of my excessive size and bulk.

Muddy stretched out her arm next to mine. I had never imagined myself to be anything other than black, but I was clearly lighter than her. 'You must be poisoned by the blood of both,' she said.

I didn't say anything.

'"I who am poisoned with the blood of both, where shall I turn, divided to the vein?" It's a poem by Derek Walcott.'

'I've never heard of him,' I responded.

'Detectives don't really think too much, do they?' she asked with a snicker.

I moved my arm away from hers. I was hurt and hated myself for feeling wounded. I had no illusions about who was in charge here. The simple truth was that she could have poured gasoline on me, struck a match and I would have stayed to see what happened. But nevertheless I had to try and get some of my questions answered. I took out the photo of Samuel Alexander we had found in the locket in the bath and placed it before her.

'Madeline ... Do you know him?'

'Call me Muddy.'

'Okay, Muddy, do you know him?'

'Yes, he was my lover.'

'How long ago?'

'A couple of years ... '

'Do you know that he's dead?' I asked.

I felt her startle. She took a few deep breaths.

'Suicide,' I said. 'With you in his hand.' It felt good being mean to her.

'You asshole, you let me sit there all night having fun without telling me?' she said bitterly.

I didn't say anything. I had nothing to say.

Reaching into her kitchen drawer, Muddy pulled out two joints and lit both of them. I started to say that I didn't smoke, but she reached for her cell, dialled and a few seconds later the watchman appeared on the other side of the barred kitchen window. She stood up and passed him one of the joints, taking a long drag on the other as she did so.

'I came here with nowhere to go, so I worked in some shitty joints,' she began. 'Then I met Sammy. It was him who introduced me to the spoken word, to The Last Poets, to the world of Saul Williams ... You know them?'

But before I could answer she started reciting something from The Last Poets; she spoke softly, yet each line felt like a muted gunshot: '"You will not be able to stay home, brother. You will not be able to plug in, turn on and cop out. You will not be able to lose yourself on skag and skip, skip out for beer during commercials, because the revolution will not be televised ... " Beautiful people with beautiful words, who found a way to express their anger and hurt.'

She paused as a tremor ran across her face, but I couldn't tell whether it was the thought of Samuel's death or the words that had moved her close to tears. 'Jesus, I loved the movie *Slam*,' she finally continued. 'I must have watched it a thousand times, and at first I tried to be like them, sound like them, until one day my voice broke, and I found the first words that were ever mine, created by me: When they cut down my roots they will find the blood of many, of friends, of lovers, of family and of enemies. Here children learn to grow into the earth and breastfeed themselves, and like death or life, my enemies feed on many cutting them down like sugar cane or weeds ... '

She stopped and laughed in embarrassment. 'Quite sloppy, but they were my first words. I had learned to speak, and I said them over and over again. It was Sammy who helped me find my voice.' She paused again. 'And I left because as soon as my voice broke I no longer liked what I saw.'

Standing up, she went to the sitting room – where I could hear her shuffling through drawers – and came back with a photo album. The photos in the album were arranged chronologically: Photographs of her as child – in primary school uniform with her parents standing stiffly behind her. Little Muddy with a slightly older brother. A sister is born. Muddy in secondary school with her friends. Then abruptly, three unmarked graves and she is in the Rwandan Patriotic Army. After that there were others of her in a makeshift hospital – her face unrecognisable, her arms in plaster. This after she was captured by the genocidaires. 'They said my looks saved me,' she said, her face hard. 'They brutalised and raped me, but they didn't kill me. Instead, they left me out in the forest to die.'

As soon as she was a little bit better she had made for Kenya. She didn't go back to the RPA – she was tired of it all, she just wanted a little bit of peace.

'Muddy, did you kill people?' I asked in spite of myself. It was a stupid question, what else could she have been doing in the RPA? It was just that I couldn't reconcile the sad woman in front of me with the hardened soldier in the photos.

'I want to show you something.'

I followed her out through the kitchen door to her backyard. She sat down on the grass and I followed her example, only to find it was wet with dew.

'Look,' she said and pointed up at the sky.

I looked up. The moon was gone and the dawn was on its way – the sky was a simmering red. It was beautiful, romantic even, except for the rather odd circumstances.

'Many nights when I was in Rwanda I would see the sky like this and see hell,' she said. 'I wanted to see stars again and breathe air that was not filled with the smell of burning human flesh. I wanted that for me, my neighbours and my country.' She paused. 'Never ask me if I have killed. You have no right. I only forgive you because you are a foreigner here,' she added, barely able to contain her anger.

'I am sorry, Muddy,' I said. 'It won't happen again.'

She accepted my apology.

'The white girl, do you know her?' I asked, knowing I was being unfair but hoping for an answer that would finally make it all make sense.

'No. Never seen her.'

'Is Joshua a killer? I mean, do you think he is capable of killing?'

She laughed sadly. 'You still don't understand, do you? The worst killers are the survivors. They know life is cheap, no matter what the rest of the world says. So, yes, Joshua can kill, but so can I or anyone else who has been through such a hell as we have.'

Silence, for the first time in my life I heard true silence. Nothing. No cars, air conditioners or heaters, no sirens or noisy drunks trying to make their way home, not even the hum of street lights, just silence.

'Look, man, I gotta teach you some Kiswahili,' Muddy said, suddenly switching the topic. 'You can't be running around here like a fool. You have to speak the people's language. I mean, you are supposed to be undercover, right?'

I welcomed her playfulness.

'*Habari? Sema. Mambo.*'

I repeated the words as best I could, but Muddy was soon beside herself with laugher. 'You sound like a princess looking for water,' she said. 'Try again. *Habari?*: hello, what's the news? *Sema*: I want to know but I also don't care. *Mambo*: I am really just announcing myself, but if you have relevant news, share.'

I tried to sound like her, but it wasn't long until she was on the grass thrashing around, trying to recover her breath. I suppose the weed might have had something to do with it.

'Tell me, man, when I speak English, do I sound to you like you sound to me?' she asked, propping herself up on her elbows.

It was at that moment that I knew for certain that there would never come a time when we would meet under different circumstances. This was it. And so, instead of answering her, I pulled myself closer and kissed her. Then, as I felt her tongue reach for mine, I broke away and began to kiss her neck. She tasted salty but I kept kissing every little bit of her I could find until she pushed me away. I watched as she stood up and pulled her dashiki over her head. Tall, naked, her long thin dreadlocks covering her breasts, she beckoned and I followed, almost tripping over my jeans as I struggled to get out of my clothes.

By the time I got to the room I was naked and had but a single thought in my head: Muddy. I did not know what to expect – I had not been with a woman in a long time – and my palms were clammy as I ran my hands over her body. We kissed again but only managed to clink our teeth together and she laughed again. Then I moved so that she came on top of me, her breasts running against my thighs and chest before she finally took charge.

Later, just as I was about to drift off to sleep, Muddy started having a nightmare, muttering over and over again: 'A word is flesh. A word is flesh, do not kill it.'

I thought of waking her, but after a few minutes her body relaxed and she went back into a peaceful sleep. I stayed up for a while after that, drifting in a space between sleep and consciousness, letting thoughts wash over me without letting them take hold – my ex-wife, blues music, Muddy, the case. Then, finally, I too drifted off.

HOW MUCH IS A GUILTY CONSCIENCE WORTH?

" I woke up very early the following morning, slid quietly out of bed and made my way to Muddy's kitchen. Once there I tried to imitate O's omelette, but it came out a jumbled mess – although with some toast and coffee we would still have a full breakfast of sorts. Finally, with everything as ready as it was ever going to be, I went to wake Muddy, but she was sleeping so peacefully that I decided to let our breakfast go cold. With nothing else to do, I unlocked her many security doors, made sure the dogs were chained up and then stepped outside for a walk.

I found the watchman milking one of Muddy's cows and, much to his delight, tried to help him, though I only succeeded in getting cow shit on my shoes. Walking it off through the small orchard behind the house I realised that I had never had an avocado straight from the tree. They tasted amazing and I ate so many of them that I thought I would get sick. Then, having finished with my makeshift breakfast, I walked around some more, fed the chickens and played with the goats. I hadn't felt so good in years.

After an hour or so, Muddy came rushing out of the house with my phone. Some nun wanted to speak to me, she said. It was about Janet. She had beaten up one of her classmates and the nun wanted me to speak to her. I had no idea what I would say to her but I wanted to help, and once I had explained the situation to Muddy she instantly agreed to come with me.

About an hour later, we arrived to find the girls at their mid-morning break. There was a lot of chatter and laughter; some girls skipping rope, others playing hand games in their bright uniforms. So Janet, who upon seeing us enter the nun's office ran to me and held on to me sobbing, was quite a contrast to the life outside. She must have been angry that for her schoolmates life was continuing, while for her it had come to a standstill.

The nun left us in her office without saying a word, and it was only then that Janet finally let go of me and I was able to introduce Muddy to her. By then I was on the brink of tears, so I was relieved when Muddy started talking to Janet. And in the course of her talking to Janet I was able to understand Muddy a little better. Muddy had survived to wake up one day alone, where the day before she had had parents, brothers and sisters. They spoke about Rwanda, people they might both have known, Rwandan music and food, before Muddy got to it: 'Sister, this is a cruel country on a cruel continent, there are no second chances. You decide here and now whether you want to live or you want to die. If you want to die a slow death, then come with us and I will find you a job working as a barmaid,' she said. 'These are your two choices. There are no others; not for you or for me. You are still alive, and that is a blessing, you should not waste it.'

Muddy sounded harsh, but she was telling Janet how it was. She had to choose to fight for her life or surrender now and accept failure.

Janet started sobbing again. She looked at me, and I looked back at her without saying anything. I wondered if she thought I might decide to take her back to the United States with me, but she must have known that it wasn't an option.

'Janet, you have to decide what you want to do right now,' Muddy said urgently. 'You have to decide before we walk out of that door.'

Janet looked at Muddy through her tears and then at me. 'I will stay. I will stay and finish,' she said, trying to sound brave.

Muddy hugged her, laughing wildly and congratulating her as if she had just graduated. I suppose for all of us there comes a time when we have to take responsibility for our lives, but Janet had had to take responsibility for hers even before she knew there was more to life than trauma after trauma.

The nun came back. Break was over and it was time for the next class, she told us. But Janet wouldn't let go of Muddy, and eventually, with no other choice, Muddy had to gently make her. The nun didn't ask what had transpired, she just wiped Janet's tears roughly from her face before opening the office door so that the girl could walk back to her class, to her life.

'The first Saturday of each month is visitors' day,' she said to Muddy as she watched Janet walk away. 'Keep coming back, okay? It is not easy for her.'

Muddy nodded in agreement and we left.

❝ It was midday by the time I dropped Muddy back at her place and the sun was beating down on me. By the time I had driven back into Nairobi again I was bathed in sweat. Nothing like a Fanta to quench your thirst, so I decided to stop at a store close to O's. There are things that Americans have long been denied – like drinking a cold Fanta straight from a glass bottle. The only problem is that to leave with the bottle you have to put down a deposit, so I just chugged it, slamming the bottle on the counter like I was in a bar. But as I opened the door to hop back into the Land Rover a massive figure materialised from nowhere. I didn't even have time to cry out before I felt the heavy blow to the back of my head.

When I regained my senses – to a pounding headache – I found myself in a dark room tied tightly to a chair. The first thing I noticed was the smell of rotting meat, then, slowly, the loud din of voices, drunken and sober, coming from somewhere nearby. I wasn't gagged but there was little point in screaming – I was in a room behind a bar somewhere, I figured, and there was no chance anyone would hear me.

After what seemed an eternity I heard the fumble of keys and padlock and the door finally opened. For a few brief moments I saw daylight, and then the room went dark as the door closed again. Seconds later a bright light came on directly above me and someone pulled up a chair and sat down heavily. He was so close that I could see his expensive leather shoes, white socks and grey trousers, but his face was outside the circle of light, hidden in the darkness.

'Who are you?' I asked angrily.

'Pardon my manners, Detective Ishmael,' a man said in an accent very much like Joshua's. 'You have been so much in my mind recently that it feels like we are old friends. My name is Abu. Abu Jamal.' There was a smile in his voice.

'What are we doing here?'

'That is not the question. The question is why are you still alive? No, don't answer. It is simple: you are alive because you still have a purpose. God kept you alive for a reason ... '

I started laughing.

'Did I say something funny?' he asked.

'You a priest?'

'No, Detective Ishmael, but I do believe that God kept you alive to return balance to our world,' he said cryptically.

Only one person had addressed me this way and that was the person whose call had brought me to Africa. He had my attention.

'Yes,' he answered my unspoken question. 'I made the call as per Mr Alexander's instructions. It seems that you were becoming a thorn in our side, as you Americans say, and you were to be invited here so that we could kill you.'

'You were supposed to get me out of the way?'

'Yes, but that is beside the point now. Things have shifted ... '

He paused to light a cigarette. I stared at him, trying to catch his face, but his hands were cupped around the light and I could only make out a receding hairline that was flecked with grey.

'Detective, allow me to come to the point ... Do you know how much guilt is worth nowadays?'

I shook my head.

'Say there is a genocide in which a million or so people die while the world watches. And say that the country in which this genocide happens ends up owning the guilt of that world, because it stood by and did nothing. How much do you think that guilt is worth?'

'Do you always speak in riddles? Just get to the point!' I said in frustration.

'Yes, it would have been a shame to kill a man who knows so little,' he said. 'All right, say you are a savvy businessman who realises that there is money to be made out of this guilt ... a lot of money. Say you have a white face, but you find a black man, a hero who helps you tap into the community of refugees from this country that owns the guilt of the world, and you start a Refugee Centre. Say you then start a foundation called Never Again to tap into this guilt all over the world.' He paused. 'Am I making any sense yet?'

Some things had begun to fall into place, although a lot more was still out of focus. This man was some sort of middleman in a corrupt corporation fronted by the Refugee Centre and the Never Again Foundation, with Samuel as the acceptable white face and noble Joshua the stirrer of that guilt. Together they had preyed on the world's conscience ever since the genocide.

'Did Joshua do the things they say he did?' I asked.

'Having met a few people who owe their lives to him, including that beautiful young woman you left Club 680 with last night, I believe so. When he was offered money and fame for his good deeds, he felt entitled to them. It was Samuel who found Joshua. But who really knows? Truth can be stranger than fiction, no?'

'Did Joshua kill the white girl?'

'You could say Mr Alexander and I were partners,

Detective Ishmael. But naturally, being black, I was the junior partner, so I do not know these things. What I do know is that there are three forces here at work: the Refugee Centre, the Never Again Foundation and Joshua. Perhaps if you shake these apple trees, as you Americans say, something will fall off.' He laughed. 'And before you ask, no, I had never seen her before.'

'How big is this thing?'

'If I told you, Detective Ishmael, you would not believe me.' His cellphone glowed in the dark as he dialled a number. A few seconds later a gorilla of a man – the same one who had hit me over the head earlier, no doubt – walked in with a briefcase which he handed to Jamal. 'Untie him,' Jamal ordered.

The giant approached wordlessly, producing a long shiny knife from a sheath along his forearm as soon as he stepped into the light. For a moment I felt panic as he walked around to stand behind me. Then I felt a tug and my hands and legs were suddenly free, the pain intense as the blood flowed back into my limbs.

As the giant left, he turned on the lights. Not in a million years would I have expected that Abu Jamal and I had already met – and only a few hours earlier too. I felt foolish and alarmed at the same time, and I broke into a short weird laugh, making a sound I had never made before me in my life – a sound of complete and utter surprise, mixed in with genuine mirth, fear, indignation and embarrassment. The man sitting before me was Samuel Alexander's manservant. The elderly man whom O had insulted on the night of Samuel's suicide.

'Nothing is what it seems, that is the truth,' he said as if he and I were sitting together, watching a secret being unveiled. 'It is okay to take a moment … you smoke?'

Without waiting for my reply he lit a cigarette for me. I noticed my hands were unsteady as I reached for it. It was not that I was afraid for my life, I was scared of what I did not know – everything had become a surprise.

'I think we just might come to an understanding,' Jamal added. He opened the briefcase that the giant had left behind and handed me a hefty folder. 'My gift to you, Detective Ishmael. All you need to know.'

I opened it and quickly glanced at the papers – it contained letters, documents from the Refugee Centre and a logbook with hundreds of names in it.

I looked up at him, alarmed. 'Did you kill Samuel?' I asked him.

'No, I had gone to retrieve these documents. You gentlemen interrupted me.'

'Why didn't you say anything?'

'I needed a moment to think. As you might be aware, things around here are changing very fast,' he explained. 'And you, I had to decide what to do about you now that Samuel was gone. Surely that was understandable.' He said it like it was something I ought to have figured out for myself.

'So what do you get in the end?' I asked.

'I want to be the last man standing. Consciences will continue to bleed money and it is time we did some good with it. I am rich. It is time for phase two: legacy building. But have no illusions, Detective Ishmael, I will put you down if needs be.'

'And the Foundation? You want a piece of it?'

'The Refugee Centre is the foundation of the Foundation,' he laughed at his own joke. 'Whoever controls the Centre controls the suffering, and whoever controls the suffering controls the guilt … See what I am getting at?'

'This shit, I have to tell you that this shit is way above my pay grade,' I told him. 'I just want to find out who killed the girl.'

He laughed again and then, with a smile, he stretched out his hand and we shook as if we were concluding a big deal.

'Some might think you a simple man, but I think you are a man of singular determination,' he said. 'Like a bulldog, as you Americans say. It's a shame I couldn't help you with that, but every little thing counts.'

'Tell me, Jamal, did you kill Samuel?' I asked him again, looking him straight in the face.

'And make it look like a suicide?' He paused. 'No. I liked Samuel … as much as one can like a fellow criminal.'

'So why did he commit suicide?'

'This is not easy work that we do, Detective Ishmael. If you are not careful it catches up to you. We all come to this work from somewhere. And we live in some very dark places. I am sorry I cannot be of more help than that,' he said apologetically, turning to leave.

I watched as Jamal made his way towards the door. Before he stepped outside he opened the briefcase and placed it gently on the floor, then he was gone.

As soon as I was able to stand I walked over to the briefcase. Inside I found my weapon, fully loaded, and my wallet, badge, cell and car keys. Opening the door I realised that I was in the middle of a meat market – which explained the smell. There were rows and rows of meat stalls interrupted only by small bars. For Kenyans, this was *nyama choma* heaven. I picked a stall randomly and used their phone to call O and tell him where I was and what had happened.

After I had finished filling O in – and told him where I had left the Land Rover – I ordered two kilos of *nyama choma* and two Tuskers – one for myself and one for O when he arrived. Then, with trembling hands, I opened the folder, sipped my Tusker and started going through the documents.

❮ How much can a guilty conscience be worth? Millions, it would seem. The logbook was a record of donations coming in and money going out. There was money coming in from all sorts of organisations – the United Nations, The World Bank – and from all sorts of governments as well, from Britain to Syria. The Ford, Rockefeller, and Bill and Melinda Gates Foundations had also given money, along with Hollywood types and sports stars. Anybody and everybody with money was in the game. This was the world trying to clear its conscience, and to do that it was prepared to pay close to seventy million dollars a year.

I turned to the recipients' page and it became clearer how the whole thing worked. Let's say Shell has ten million dollars due in taxes. Under normal circumstances Shell could give that money to charity – thus not paying the tax and at the same time creating publicity and goodwill for itself. But what was happening was that Shell would give the ten million to the Never Again Foundation, which in turn kicked six million back to the Shell board, keeping four million for itself. The six million went into the private accounts of the board and the four million to Samuel Alexander and his subordinates. It was such a neat cycle, that each year generated so many millions for CEOs and wealthy philanthropists, that it might as well have been legal. The rich had found a way of giving back to themselves.

And the money from the non-corrupt, from those who gave because they wanted to educate a child orphaned by the genocide, these little donations also amounted to millions – and the money generated was not going to the refugees. On paper, this money was buying cars and houses for the Refugee Centre, but it was surely going into buying favours, keeping politicians silent and into private bank accounts. There was no way any of this money was making it to the refugees I had seen in Mathare.

There were some African names on the payroll that didn't make sense to me, so I turned to the letters and e-mails as I waited for O. They were from all over the world. To clean up the millions the Never Again Foundation and the Refugee Centre had to have little offices wherever there were Rwandan refugees to be found. And in some of those places their representatives had made deals that for whatever reason had gone bad. Some of the e-mails were from these representatives, demanding money and threatening to go public if it wasn't forthcoming. There were also e-mails from several CEOs, asking for their cut. These were politely written but the threat behind them was unmistakable – one ended with the line, 'hospitality begets hospitality'. There was also one cold e-mail from Joshua to Samuel reminding him there was honour amongst thieves and that 'the five hundred thousand' was long overdue. Had Samuel Alexander been scheming the other schemers?

Whatever was going on, one thing was clear, the Refugee Centre and the Never Again Foundation had spread themselves too thin. Collapse was almost inevitable. Was this why Samuel had committed suicide and left an apology for Joshua? Was Jamal hoping that with Samuel now dead and Joshua exposed, and in a US jail, he could resuscitate the Refugee Centre and use it for his own ends? And what did any of this have to do with the white girl? Had she simply stumbled onto something she shouldn't have?

'I have been looking all over for you, and you have been eating *nyama choma*?' O asked incredulously, pulling up a chair and grabbing a Tusker off the counter.

I showed him the bump on the back of my head and filled him in on the fine details I hadn't told him over the phone – including our visit to Janet and the real identity of Samuel's man Friday.

'Shit, I knew something wasn't quite right with that old man, he couldn't hide his dignity,' O said, trying to justify his misjudgement.

'It doesn't matter,' I told him, pushing the logbook across the bar towards him. 'This is more important ... Take a look at this.'

'What you have here is our death sentence,' O said as he looked at the names on the recipients' page. 'This is our Minister for Internal Security, this is a Member of Parliament ... ' And he went on as he scrolled down the list of names.

'That means we have to move fast,' I said.

'What do you suggest?' O asked.

It was time to blow this whole thing open. My logic was very simple: it doesn't matter how good you are, stay in a gunfight long enough and eventually you will get shot. We couldn't keep outrunning death. We had to give those involved something else to think about.

'We have to hit them where it hurts the most,' I told O, trying to feel hopeful. 'We go after their reputations. If we can get the story out there it will get us some protection.'

We left for O's office where I called the Chief, explained the situation, and faxed the papers to him.

'Oh, boy, don't I miss black-on-black crime,' the Chief said when he rang back twenty minutes later. 'Listen, Ishmael, if this is what takes us down, then so be it. But you have to make it count. I am with you, but all you have here are some documents from some shady African crime figure. We are up against power itself ... you understand me?' He paused. 'We need to tie all this shit to the white girl. You want to bring these guys down? Connect them to the white girl ... she has one angry ghost.'

I understood what he meant – the rage surrounding her death was such that anyone involved in it was going to go down no matter how powerful they were. The Never Again Foundation and Refugee Centre would tumble down once the face of their victim was the white girl's. Were we manipulating race? The calculation was simple: one million lives did not move the world, African countries included, to intervene, but the death of one beautiful blonde girl would. We did not create that equation – we found it as it was. And we would use it to get justice.

'And, Ishmael?'

'Yes, Chief?'

'You need to get your black ass home. Shit here has hit the fan and it's spilling all over me,' he said and hung up.

At least I had his backing. Maybe he had finally tired of playing politics and wanted to do something real for a change.

With the Chief on board I called Mo and faxed the papers to her. I waited for about ten minutes then called her again. 'Did you get your Pulitzer material?' I asked her, trying to keep things light.

'Yeah ... Two days, gimme two days,' she said, sounding serious. 'I need at least two to put this shit together. I wanna look into the Never Again Foundation, they stink bad.'

'Call the Chief if you need anything,' I told her. 'Tell him I sent you.'

'Sure thing ... ' She paused. 'And, babe, get out of this alive, you hear?' she added.

We had two days to survive. Once the story was out, we would be safer. But by the same token everyone would be scared to talk to us. So we also had two days in which to make something happen. It was nine pm. We sat around the office talking about the case, trying to figure out what to do next.

'I keep going back to Madeline. Look, man, she knew Samuel Alexander and she knows Joshua. She is the connection, she has to know something,' O finally said.

'I spoke with her last night ... nothing ... '

'You mean you questioned her?' O asked sceptically. 'Was that before or afterwards?'

I gave him an angry glare, but deep down I knew he was right.

'Brother, you are getting everything mixed up. That is

all I am saying,' O said. 'Maybe she's not hiding something, maybe she is. Maybe she doesn't know she has something we can use. Use your head, man. We have to talk to her.'

❝ We got to Madeline's at about ten thirty. She was in her pyjamas, getting ready for bed, and was not very happy to see us, especially after we explained why we were there.

'Listen, Madeline, I am not saying you are hiding anything,' O tried to explain, 'but you are the only person we know who knew both Joshua and Samuel.'

'Your friend is a fucking asshole,' Muddy said, turning to me. 'For one, I did not know Joshua that well ... '

'I am not saying you were fucking him,' O said defensively.

'He's right, Muddy,' I added, 'we're not saying you're mixed up in anything, but you might know something without even ... '

'Like what?' she snapped at me.

'We spent a whole day in Mathare trying to find someone who might have known Joshua, but no one would tell us anything. They wouldn't even admit that they knew about the Refugee Centre. Why is that?' I asked, sounding every bit the cop.

She put her hands over her face. 'I don't know ... Maybe someone had threatened them?'

'What about the Never Again Foundation?' I asked.

'What about it? The Refugee Centre is the left hand, the Foundation is the right.'

'What about Joshua and women?' I asked.

'He used to specialise in girls from his school,' she said

bitterly, 'but these days ... I have no idea.'

O opened the briefcase and handed her the letters and logbook. She looked at him in surprise, then began to leaf through the letters, whistling every now and then in surprise at what she was reading. Finally, she put them aside and started working her way through the logbook. But with each flip of the page my disappointment grew – it was clear that Muddy really did not know anything that could help us. I went and stood by the kitchen window, trying to think of where else we could look.

'Kokomat, look ... Kokomat is listed,' Muddy suddenly yelled in excitement.

I rushed back to the dining room. She was pointing at an entry: Kokomat Supermarket. They had received one million dollars from the Never Again Foundation.

'So?' O asked. 'That is just one of many Kenyan companies listed.'

'And you are supposed to be the fucking detectives ... ' Muddy rolled her eyes at us. 'Kokomat is one of the biggest supermarket chains in Nairobi! They should be giving money to the Foundation, not getting it from them.'

We still looked puzzled.

'And it is owned by a Rwandan women's cooperative,' Muddy explained. 'They are being paid to keep quiet about something.'

This was something! Muddy stood up and I kissed her hard. Would she come with us to Kokomat to help us find out where the women lived? O asked. She agreed and went to put on a light sweater. Then, together, we hopped into the Land Rover and drove off.

❝ The massive gates of the main Kokomat offices were closed, which wasn't a surprise considering the time of night. Undeterred, Muddy climbed out of the Land Rover and approached the security guard. She chatted with him for a few seconds before reaching into her back pocket for some money and what was clearly a joint. Minutes later she was back with the directions – the owners lived in Muthaiga. Of course they lived in Muthaiga, I thought, the estate was a cesspool of wealth.

It was close to midnight but we couldn't wait till morning and twenty minutes later we were in Muthaiga, O showing his badge at gate after gate until we were finally outside the address we had been given. Muddy said it was better if she went in alone and with reluctance we agreed. She was an insider, no matter how much of an outsider she seemed.

A middle-aged woman opened the front door and she and Muddy spoke animatedly for about ten minutes, then she looked back at us before walking into the house. We sat outside for another half an hour, then, just as I was about to go looking for Muddy, chauffeur-driven black Benzes started pulling up. We counted five in all, and out of each popped a middle-aged woman dressed in long, flowing African clothes. They must live in Muthaiga as well, I thought as I watched Muddy and the owner of the house welcome the arrivals.

'What the hell is going on?' O asked.

'This is your country, you tell me,' I replied, just as intrigued as he was.

'My country, yes, but here we are both foreigners,' he scoffed.

After another half an hour or so the front door opened

again and the owner of the house called us inside. She led us to the sitting room where we found the five women and Muddy – out of place with her jeans and dreadlocks. The owner of the house introduced herself. Her name was Mary Karuhimbi from Rwanda and she was the Managing Director of Kokomat (the five women were the top-ranking executives at the supermarket). Mary Karuhimbi then went on to give us the names of her parents and grandparents and her clan name. Everyone followed suit, even O. When it was my turn, I named my parents and grandparents but apologised for not having a clan name. Ms Karuhimbi waved away my apology. 'No need for sorry,' she said, 'sometime brothers and sisters have different mothers and fathers.'

Then Mary Karuhimbi called Muddy over so that she could translate for her. I felt the butterflies in my stomach. Finally we were onto something. This was it.

'My daughter, yes, I can call her my daughter, says that you risked your lives to save a young girl in Mathare,' Muddy translated. 'We thank you for that because she is one of our own. We owe you a debt. We will repay you tonight with the truth.

'She also says that that Joshua Hakizimana might have taken the life of a young white woman. And that you, our long-lost son, seek justice for her. We also thank you for that. It does not matter whether it is one of our own, or one of theirs, a young life anywhere is an important life because it is the future. We claim her death as the death of one of our own.

'Investigators Ishmael and Odhiambo, we have spoken amongst ourselves ... Harsh words were exchanged between us, but we have decided that even if it was Jesus who had committed such a crime we would have to speak out.'

O and I looked at each other, unsure of protocol. Should we thank them? But before either of us could muster the courage to say anything she had ploughed on, Muddy trailing in her wake as she struggled to translate quickly enough for O and me.

'You want to know about Joshua the hero?' Mary Karuhimbi spat on the immaculate tiled floor. 'That is Joshua, your hero,' she said angrily, pointing at her spit.

I hadn't been expecting her to say nice things about Joshua, but outright hatred? I was surprised.

'We are all from the same village. Survivors ... But sometimes I am so numb that I do not know if I am still alive,' Muddy continued as Mary Karuhimbi began speaking again. 'Is there redemption in such suffering as ours? Can hell be any worse? Ah, can even heaven make all this worthwhile?'

Not knowing what to say O and I just nodded for her to continue.

'When we first heard whispers that there was a headmaster who had turned his school into a sanctuary we were filled with hope. The violence was like a flood, and when it reached the outskirts of our village we resolved to search for higher ground. Having heard of Joshua Hakizimana's school we naturally resolved to go there. There were about two hundred of us, and since we could not all go at once, blindly, we first sent my son to find a way to the school, talk to the headmaster and tell him that we needed his help. My son was gone for three days, but he returned with exactly what we had hoped for: the permission of the headmaster and a map that we were to follow.

'It would not be easy, he told us. We would have to walk through the forest, hiding ourselves from anyone we might encounter along the way. And just in case we were stopped, we were, the headmaster had told my son, to tell the butchers: "We are the children of Moses." Then the sea of violence would part. The headmaster had even given my son a wad of francs to bribe our way through in case the secret code failed. Joshua Hakizimana had given us a way out; we would not fail him.

'We took our elderly, our sick and the children and started our journey. It was slow. We could only manage about fifteen kilometres a day, but we kept moving. Finally, we could see the school. It was on top of a hill, about half a day's walk from where we were. But before we could get there we walked right into a trap. We should have known ... Why was there a clearing in the middle of a forest? But we were excited, and more than that we trusted the map drawn by the hand of the headmaster.

'We found ourselves surrounded by young men, who just days earlier would have called me mother. They asked for the leader and I raised my hand. I in turn asked for their leader, and he stepped from the crowd holding his machete as if he was simply going to his plot of land to garden.

'"We are the children of Moses," I whispered to him.

'He asked me to repeat what I had told him out loud as he had nothing to hide from his troops. "We are the children of Moses," I repeated. And that was when they started laughing.

'Unsure of what to do, I collected whatever valuables we had carried with us and offered them to him in addition to the money from the school. He took our jewellery, thanking me and telling me that it would look good on their pure-blood wives, then he took the wad of money and for a moment it looked like they were going to let us go. But what he said next stopped us from gathering our belongings.

'"The old man always uses the same wad of notes," he said to his boys. There was more laughter and the young men encircling us moved a little closer, some of them raising their machetes in the air.

'"My son, what do you mean?" I asked

'"How can I be your son, you old bitch?" He laughed in my face. "How can your blood run in my veins? You are only fit to wash my mother's feet. You hear?"

'I apologised again and again. I had no pride. I just wanted my children to live.

'"The headmaster uses honey to trap the ants," he said, waving the money up in the air.

'The circle was getting tighter and we huddled together. I looked back at my son. I wanted to catch his eye so that he knew that I loved him, but he was too scared to do anything but stare blindly at the young men. By now almost everyone was crying out: "We are the children of Moses. We are the children of Moses."

'"What do you mean? I don't understand," I yelled at the young man in front of me.

'"You don't understand? Then find out in hell!" he said.

'The last thing I remember was the flash of his machete.'

Mary Karuhimbi removed her headscarf to reveal a deep scar that ran across the side of her head, so deep that no hair grew there.

'My son did not make it ... ' Muddy said, her voice filled

with emotion as Mary Karuhimbi continued. 'The school was the honey, and we were the ants. Only a handful of us, left for dead, survived.'

It made perfect sense. The black Schindler, as the media had called him, had saved a few in order to use them as bait and reel in whole villages searching for refuge. It was a brilliant set-up because no one would have expected such evil, especially from a man who a few weeks earlier had been educating their children. I had met rapists and murderers, but this kind of evil was something else. It takes a cold heart filled with nothing but contempt for others to do what Joshua had done. And it takes a strong will not only to continue living, but to also enjoy life. How could a human being who has slaughtered thousands continue living, and even flourish as Joshua had done? Now I was beginning to get him in focus I knew that he had killed the white girl. I just didn't know why yet.

I rushed outside to throw up but nothing came out. As I leant against the wall of the house, trying to pull myself together, I remembered Lord Thompson's words: 'To catch ants, you use honey,' he had said just before O had shot him. 'You use honey to catch ants.' Did he know? Was this what he was trying to tell us? Surely it was too much of a coincidence that he and Mary Karuhimbi would use the same words?

I went back inside where the women were sobbing quietly. O was sitting with his hand on that of Mary Karuhimbi.

'Mother, when it was all over, how come you did not report him?' O asked.

'My son, who would have believed us?' she answered, Muddy still translating. 'I have seen his evil, but can I take that to court? It almost killed us when we went to the Foundation and they offered us money to keep quiet. We knew we could do a lot of good with it, and that is what we tried to do, but now another person is dead because of our silence.'

She waited for the other women to nod in agreement.

'Detective Ishmael, we want to hire your services,' Mary Karuhimbi finally continued, looking in my direction as the women reached into their purses and each produced several large wads of hundred dollar bills. 'This is three hundred thousand dollars,' she said as they passed the money to her and she piled it up neatly in front of me on the coffee table. 'You have our blessing. Let the beast walk this earth no more.'

A few thousand dollars laid out like that looks manageable. Three hundred thousand looks a lot more scary and a lot more tempting. Every detective, when offered a bribe, thinks about it – two thousand dollars, no one will probably ever know; three hundred thousand and the risk of getting caught is worth it. I thought about everything I could do with the money. I could buy a house and still have a lot of change left over. Muddy and I could leave Kenya and set up shop on some island I had never heard of. But this would be no ordinary bribe, if there is ever such a thing – a million people had died and I wasn't going to become part of yet another secret related to the genocide.

'This cycle has to end,' I said as I shook my head. 'I swear to you that I'll get him for the murder of the white girl, but I won't kill for money.'

The women looked over at O, who after some silence smiled and also declined.

'Then, my sons, you have what you came for,' Mary

Karuhimbi said as she stood up to walk us out. 'Now you know Joshua.'

At the front door she gave O and me a brief hug, but she held on to Muddy for a long time. I wondered how someone could be as wounded and as wronged as Mary Karuhimbi and yet still be so dignified and loving.

Finally, breaking away, Muddy thanked her and we left.

Somewhere on the way to Muddy's, I said jokingly that Mary Karuhimbi reminded me of my mother.

'Is she also corrupt?' Muddy asked, to O's obvious amusement. But I could tell I had spoken for them too. Sometimes, no matter how hardened we are by life, we miss places where we once felt warm, safe and wanted – and if such a place never existed we made it up.

❮ 'Did you know his last name, Hakizimana, means "God saves"? Now there is some irony,' Muddy said bitterly.

We were lying in her bed idly, lacing our fingers together.

'Did you have any idea?' I asked her.

'No, but now that I know it makes sense. There was always something about him …' her voice trailed off, but I knew exactly what she meant.

'I understand about the bribe,' she said a couple of minutes later. 'You're right, there is too much blood on the money, but you have to do something about Joshua.'

I agreed, but unless I was able to tie him to the murdered girl he was going to get away with yet another murder, and after almost a week in Kenya I still had no idea who she was. What I did have, however, was enough to rattle his cage – I now knew who he was and what he had done in Rwanda.

I talked it over with Muddy and then called O. They both were in agreement – there was nothing more for me to do in Kenya, it was time for me to return to the United States. The key now was Joshua. I called the Chief from Muddy's, and when he called me back I explained the situation. After I was done he agreed that whatever else we needed would have to come from Joshua and he confirmed that he would arrange me a seat on a flight the following afternoon. There was no time to think about what Africa had come to mean to me. I was trying to solve a murder – I had followed a lead to the continent and now it was time to try and rattle my main suspect.

I hoped that Muddy and I would work something out. We just had to keep talking. I told myself that between Skype, e-mails and jet planes she might as well be a state away. If we both wanted it, we could make it work, somehow.

Just before nine am O knocked on Muddy's door. I hadn't been expecting him until midday, but he wanted to take me to Maasailand before we left for the airport. I did not protest – I was going to get to be a tourist after all. No breakfast, only a hurried kiss from Muddy, and I was back in the Land Rover.

As we pulled up to Muddy's gate her guitarist was just coming in, driving a beaten-up Toyota, his guitar in the back seat. We pulled over, so that he could pull through, and as he drew alongside he paused to chat for a minute or so. As we drove off I decided I envied him. His life was all about expression and passion, whereas mine was about giving the dead one last word – justice. Oh, well, without people like me and O, there would be no people like him, I concluded by way of consolation.

We drove through Limuru, then Nairobi, way past the airport and about an hour or so later we were in Maasailand. Every now and then we came across young Maasai boys, who looked very much like they do in the magazines, herding cattle along the roads. Finally, we came to a Maasai village. Here there were some young Maasai men milling around dressed in red sheets with their hair braided and dyed red. Taller than the average Kenyan, they were nevertheless mostly around my height – the only difference being that my frame was huge in comparison. It is the slimness that gives the Maasai their extra-tall look. As to be expected, there were some white tourists taking photographs, alternately dishing out candy and money.

'There was this story in the *Daily Nation* sometime back of a Kenyan woman who went to India, as a tourist,' O said as we watched the white tourists. 'Don't ask me why India when there is the Bahamas ... Anyway, in the Indian villages that she passed through they had never seen a black person, let a lone a black tourist with dreadlocks. They followed her in droves, some touching her skin, others tugging at her locks. She said she became the tourist attraction and the villagers the tourists. It's almost the same here,' O said, pointing at the tourists who were laughing and gesturing at the Maasai, who were in turn watching them in amusement. 'Look at that.'

We kept walking until we came to a mud hut, a manyatta. It looked more like a clay Winnebago without wheels but I did not say that to O. Urban chaos and poverty, these were things that I could relate to – it was within my experience, even when as extreme as it was in Kenya – but the Maasai and their manyattas, that was the first time I had ever been confronted with a completely different culture to mine – whatever that was. True, my first instinct was not to take photographs and buy trinkets – I did not view the Maasai as if they were wildlife – but I would be lying to say that I did not feel a wonderment that was also condescension, summed up in one thought: How can a people live like this in the twenty-first century? But even as the thought popped into my head I realised that it is exactly this kind of thinking that forms the building blocks of hate.

'Did you know that the women build the houses around here?' O asked, interrupting my thoughts as he stopped at the door to the manyatta. Then, before I could respond, he said something in Kiswahili and an elderly female voice answered. We were obviously welcome, and without another word I followed O inside.

Once my eyes had adjusted to the darkness the first things I made out were a number of framed photographs of a game warden, most of them taken out in the forests and bushland. In one the game warden was posing: gun pointed at the photographer, at his feet the carcass of an elephant with bloody stumps where its tusks had been. The warden was smiling, and I imagined that when he and his fellow wardens caught up with the poachers they would have posed over their dead bodies in exactly the same way.

Turning away from the photographs I made out an old woman, whom I took to be the mother of the slain warden, lying in bed. O spoke to her and she nodded and swallowed whatever it is that toothless old people chew all the time. I heard him mention Lord Thompson's name several times, then the old woman started smiling at O, her glassy eyes filling with tears. With great effort she managed to get out of bed and hold O, who just sat there impassively, his hands still on his knees. Finally, she pulled away and walked to the photographs of her son. She picked up one of them and held it to her chest even as she gestured to O, beckoning him to take it. But O just smiled and walked out.

The old woman hobbled to where I was and pressed the photograph to my chest, lifting up my hands one at a time to my chest so that I embraced it. She ululated several times, sobbing and laughing – she had justice at last, but her son was still dead.

❝ O asked me for the warden's photograph as he drove back to town. He looked at it; holding it in one hand, steering with the other.

'The old woman said, "My hands are burnt, my heart died with my son, my tears will not bring him back, but for justice alone I am happy to shed these tears…"' O said, his voice shaking with emotion. 'I will tell you how that makes me feel: if I went to hell and found those fuckers there, I would kill them all over again.'

The old woman was right. Justice is always after the fact, but justice after the fact is still justice and it counted as something, if only as a final act of love from those left behind. Lord Thompson, given his age, would have died soon enough, but, for O, Lord Thompson's life was worth taking so that the old woman could die with a semblance of closure.

A semblance, because full closure demands the participation of society – in the guise of judge and jury. But that wasn't an option, and from the moment Lord Thompson had been acquitted of the second murder charge O had understood that he would kill him. He had been waiting for the right moment, and if he could wait for several years until an opportunity presented itself, then he would have also rehearsed whatever guilt one might feel for killing a man like Lord Thompson out of his system.

'As a kid I wanted to be a singer,' O said, handing the photo of the game warden back to me and breaking into an off-key version of *Billie Jean*. 'But that did not go down too well,' he continued in response to my laughter. 'I got kicked out of choir when I was five.'

And with that we were onto the next item on our agenda – getting me to the airport. We made it back to O's place just in time for a late lunch, after which I called Muddy and told her where we were. She, in turn, called a cab while I packed quickly, and as soon as she arrived we were on our way to the airport.

THE ROAD TO HELL AND REVELATIONS

❝ O was driving, I was sitting in the passenger seat and Muddy was sitting between us. Anyone seeing us would probably have thought we were old college friends off to a reunion, especially as once again Kenny Rogers was blasting through the squeaky speakers, Muddy and O singing along happily. We were happy with ourselves and with life. For the first time it looked like we might not only survive the case but also break it. All I needed was to get Joshua a little rattled. My phone rang. It was a Nairobi number that I didn't know. I answered. It was Abu Jamal, and even before I heard what he had to say I knew it was going to be bad news.

'Listen, man, you are in hot soup, as you Americans say,' he began.

In spite of his convoluted way of speaking there was an urgency in his voice and I immediately turned down the Kenny Rogers so that I could hear him properly. O and Muddy started to protest but the look on my face silenced them.

'What are you saying, Jamal?' I asked. 'I'm on my way

out?'

'Look behind you.'

I looked at the traffic behind us in the wing mirror but could see nothing out of the ordinary.

'You see a beautiful Alfa Romeo five or so cars behind you?' Jamal asked. 'That is me.'

'Very nice, but why the fuck are you following us?'

'Business makes strange bedfellows, as you Americans say. Do you see the red Peugeot two cars behind you?'

'Yes.'

'Do you see the Range Rover behind it?'

'Yes.'

'Those are the bad guys, okay ... the really bad guys,' he said.

'And who are the really bad guys?' I asked, trying to match his calmness.

'You have become a man of many enemies. If we are both alive in a few hours we can sit down, have a beer and exchange notes, but for now, do as I say: pull over at the next opportunity.' He hung up.

'Not sure how Jamal got my number but he says we are being tailed ... Red Peugeot and Range Rover,' I reported. But even as I finished speaking I remembered that Abu Jamal had had my wallet and cellphone for several hours after his giant had knocked me out.

There was a service station just ahead of us. We slowed down to pull in and the two cars, each containing four men, whizzed by. As they passed us I tried to make out their faces, but all I could really see was that the occupants were almost all white – only the Peugeot had a black man in the back, his

Rasta hat clearly visible through the back window. Seconds later Jamal's Alfa Romeo, containing the man himself and three bodyguards, also whizzed by without him even as much as looking at us. I started to call the Nairobi number that had registered in my cell to tell him he was wrong – the men in the Range Rover and the Peugeot were probably white tourists; they had not even slowed down or looked in our direction – but O stopped me. 'If they are following us they are not stupid,' he said. 'Let's get back on the road and see what happens.'

'It could be Jamal setting us up,' I suggested.

'No, he would not have announced himself. Let's play it out,' O countered.

I suggested we leave Muddy behind but she wouldn't hear of it. If they were following us then they probably knew we were going to the airport, she argued. And they would know we knew something was up if we left her in the middle of nowhere.

While we decided what to do we filled the tank and O rummaged through the trunk until, from beneath the spare wheel, he produced a vest. He gave it to Muddy who expertly strapped it over her sweater. Earlier, while I was busy packing, I had given my vest to O to replace his ruined one – I was leaving for the US and I hadn't thought I'd need it again.

'Ah, the king and queen have to the protected,' O joked, slapping his hand against my vest and laughing at the situation.

I couldn't very well take my vest back. Besides, I literally owed him my life – twice.

After thirty minutes or so back on the road the same two cars were behind us again. They must have pulled over somewhere and waited for us.

'My friends, let us not wait for the fat lady to sing, eh,' Jamal said when he called again. 'Would you rather have a Range Rover or a Peugeot?' Somewhere along the way he had changed cars and he was now tailing us in a black Mercedes-Benz.

As far as I was concerned we were screwed either way. I asked O what he thought. We were in an old Land Rover and would never outrun the Range Rover, he confirmed. But even though the smaller car was much faster than us we could probably bully it off the road.

'And we will be firing down on it,' Muddy added.

'Peugeot,' I said to Jamal, feeling a familiar tightness coming over my chest.

'Follow my lead then,' Jamal said. 'And, my friend, good luck.'

Things are different when you have more than your own life to lose, and not just any life but that of someone you care about deeply. I found myself silently praying for Muddy's safety. I reached out for her hand.

'I am not a little girl, you fucking idiot,' she said fiercely, pushing my hand away. 'Give me a weapon.'

Fuck it, she's right, I thought. Chances were that she had seen more violence than either O or I ever would.

'Now I really like her,' O said to no one in particular as he reached underneath his seat and produced a 9mm that I immediately recognised as belonging to one of the hoodlums from Mathare.

Muddy removed the magazine, checked it and slapped it back in, then she took the safety off and casually advised me to do the same. Sound advice for no sooner had I prepared my weapon than we heard a loud bang followed by AK-47 fire. Jamal had pounced, and we looked back to see him and his bodyguards firing into the Range Rover. Immediately the Peugeot lurched forward and hurtled towards us, expertly weaving past the cars separating us.

I hate the moments before the action, but once it starts I am okay, I can think and act fast – sometimes. I fired through the back window so that it shattered, spraying the Peugeot with glass, then I fired again, making two neat holes through their windscreen, but despite my best efforts it stayed on our tail as we dodged in and out of traffic.

Muddy shouted for me to cover her, and I emptied my Glock into the Peugeot as she slipped through the divider into the back of the Land Rover. The Peugeot veered dangerously across the road to try and avoid the hail of bullets, but as soon as Muddy had pulled up the spare tyre to use as cover the driver steadied the car, sped up and moved alongside us. AK-47 fire tore into the Land Rover as one of the men in the back tried to shoot the tyres on the driver's side. It wasn't long before they gave way to the rims, pulling the Land Rover into the Peugeot and driving them off the road. O tried to keep going, but we all knew that there was no way we were going to make it – the Peugeot was back on the road and rapidly gaining on us.

With nothing left to lose O sped up and just at the moment when it looked like he was going to lose control, he spun the Land Rover so that it stopped with its length blocking the road. Jumping out, we took cover behind it: Muddy on one side and me on the other, with O behind the body of the Land

Rover. The Peugeot stopped. If they stepped out of the car, to make it four against three, we stood a chance. Instead it revved up before furiously shooting forward, gaining speed as it approached us. They were going to ram the Land Rover, forcing us to scatter into the open. We fired rapidly at the Peugeot but it doggedly sped towards us.

As I quickly reloaded I saw Muddy step out from behind the Land Rover, take one step forward, so that her right foot was slightly in front of her left, and lower the 9mm. I panicked, thinking she was trying to sacrifice herself to give O and me a chance, but then I saw her lift the weapon again and take aim. She stood very still for what seemed like an eternity – the bullets striking the ground around her – then, finally, I saw her hand kick up. Inside the Peugeot the driver's head snapped backwards and the car immediately went into a slide, ramming into the Land Rover. I dived out of the way, rolling to my knees, but even as I did so I saw Muddy flying backwards into the air. She had been hit.

I crept towards the car that was now a mixture of mangled metal, broken glass and blood. Both the driver and the front passenger were dead, but the white and black gunmen in the back seat were both still alive. I shot the white gunman because he was closest to me and as far as I could tell the least badly injured. Immediately, the black gunman started yelling at me not to kill him, but I wasn't planning to – I needed some information. I ordered him out of the car, and, yelling in pain, he tried to comply before he fell heavily to the ground. Instinct told me that he was pretending, but I still started to rush around the car, diving to the ground at the last minute – if he had a weapon I knew he would be aiming high. He tried to adjust but he was too slow. I fired once, hitting him in the stomach, and he slammed against the car.

It was as I was getting up to finish him off that I realised that he looked vaguely familiar. He must have picked up on my reaction because he reached up weakly and removed the Rasta hat. His dreadlocks unravelled. It was the musician; Muddy's guitarist. I was seized by rage, and I started to squeeze the trigger, but then I heard Muddy's voice shouting at me to stop.

When I got to her Muddy was on her knees, doubled over in pain by the side of the road. It was a good thing she had been wearing O's vest, otherwise she would almost certainly not have made it. It was also a good thing she had talked me out of leaving her back at the service station, I thought as I helped her to her feet, otherwise O and I would definitely not have made it. O! Looking around I saw that he was also getting slowly getting to his feet.

'Why are you here?' Muddy asked the guitarist as soon as we made it back to the Peugeot. 'Who sent you? It's too late ... just speak.'

'Joshua. It was Joshua,' the musician sobbed. 'Why are you trying to destroy him? Only the American was supposed to die.'

He must have been very stupid or have thought we were – AK-47s are not for targeted assassinations, and it was obvious to everyone that Muddy, O and I were all supposed to die.

'How did they know where to find us?' I asked, then suddenly remembered having met him earlier that morning at the gate to Muddy's house.

'I told him ... I trusted him,' Muddy said, looking down

at him.

The guitarist looked away, wiping the sweat from his face with a bloodied hand.

'Either you or him, Muddy. We put him in jail and he will be back on the streets in no time,' O said to Muddy as he hobbled up to us. It was as if he was giving a golfing partner a tip. 'End it now.'

'It was just for the money. Let me go, you have to let me go,' the guitarist pleaded with us even as he struggled for breath. 'I have a life ... songs ... I have many songs. Muddy, please, tell them, I have many songs.'

'You had no business being here,' Muddy told him coldly. 'I trusted you like no one else in my life.'

'How do you know it was Joshua?' I asked him.

'Look, look at this ... I will testify.' He handed me a bloody MoneyGram receipt from his shirt pocket. It was for one hundred thousand Kenyan shillings. The sender's name was Joshua Hakizimana and the money had been sent from Chicago, a mere two-and-half hour drive from Madison. But what would that prove? Chicago was a big city and no one in those kinds of cheque-cashing places ever asked for ID. The money could have come from anyone – the musician had nothing.

'Do you know anything about the girl?' I asked him, hoping for his own sake that he had something tangible. My rage had dissipated, but Muddy's anger was palpable.

'Look, man, you can get him with that, can't you?' the guitarist asked, half in hope and half in doubt. 'I swear you can get him with that. His bank account, you can trace it ... That is a lot of money, isn't it?'

Looking over at Muddy I shook my head, wanting to ask her to let him go but not knowing how to begin. 'You were willing to kill us for two thousand dollars, that is all this means,' I said sadly, rolling up the MoneyGram receipt into a little ball and throwing it back at him.

As if in response Muddy lifted her 9mm and pointed it at the guitarist's head. Trembling, he put his hands together as if he wanted to say a prayer, then, as Muddy hesitated, he started to sing softly. 'Well, I wish I was a catfish, swimmin' in an oh, deep, blue sea,' he sang, looking first at O and then at me. 'I would have all you good-lookin' women fishin', fishin' after ...'

But just as I thought something would give, or that we would at least see something worth saving in the guitarist or in ourselves, Muddy shot him in the head. She did not even let him finish the verse.

Surely we could have let him live – threatened him with death if we ever saw him again, whatever. I sank to the ground and covered my face in my hands, tired and hopeless. People had just died and there was no reason why we were alive other than the fact that we had more experience and better training than the four we had just killed. I lifted up my face, expecting to find a different woman in front of me than the Muddy I knew. I expected to find her transformed into something ugly, a cold killer with cold eyes, but she was still the same beautiful woman and I still loved her. Nothing made sense.

A few minutes later Jamal's black Mercedes limped up to the wreckage, the giant and another of his men dead in the back seat.

'Really nice to see you again, old man,' O said to Jamal,

breaking off from searching the bodies in the Peugeot for identification.

'I have no doubt about that, my brother,' Jamal said, climbing out of the battered Benz.

'Do you know who sent them?' I asked him, gesturing towards the three dead white men. Dressed in expensive business suits, they were clearly American, but I already knew that we would find nothing on them to tie them to Joshua or the Foundation. But where else could they have come from?

'Them white boys, they are Foundation men, straight from the US,' Jamal confirmed.

'Joshua or the Foundation?' O asked him.

'I have no idea. We are in the middle of a civil war right now, and they could have been sent by anyone, but they are Foundation men ...'

'How did you know?' I asked.

'The guitarist was their contact,' Jamal said, cocking his head as the sound of police sirens came to us from further down the road. 'He came to me thinking I was with them. He just couldn't keep from singing.' He laughed at his own witticism and hopped back into his wrecked Mercedes. 'Travel well, my friend,' he told me as he started the engine.

'I hope to God I never run into that asshole again,' O said as Jamal drove away. 'He scares me.'

What O didn't say was that we both knew Jamal would collect on the debt we owed him, and when that day came we would have to pay – he had just saved our lives.

« Back at O's place – after a brief visit to the station and another short session with the Director of Investigations – O and Muddy decided between them that it would be best if I left through Uganda. It was obvious that the Foundation would do everything in its power to prevent me getting to the airport – we had been lucky once, but we might not be so lucky again. The plan was simple enough. We would hire a car, drive all night and most of the next day before stopping at a village called Butere, which was close to the Ugandan border. Muddy had a friend who lived there. She hadn't seen her in years, but was sure we would be welcome. At the village, we would get some rest, then closer to my flight time we would slip across the border under cover of darkness.

We drove, taking turns every two hours. Sometimes I fell into a deep dreamless sleep and woke to find either O or Muddy smoking up a storm. At other times, as O drove, Muddy would slip into the back and we would make out or rest against each other. And at other times I drove, feeling as if in returning to the US I was leaving myself behind. It was almost as if the America I was going to seemed to slip further and further away the closer we got to the border.

There was a lot of time to think, and I found my mind returning again and again to what had happened on the road to the airport only a few hours earlier. I had killed based on the calculation that it was better to take one man alive than two. On top of that I had calculated that the less injured man was more of a threat and less likely to talk. Based on these calculations, calculations that I would never have thought myself capable of before I came to Africa, I had shot the white gunman. If I had waited less than two minutes Muddy would have come, and in another three O, and in ten Jamal. Not that this would have saved the guitarist or the white gunman –

they certainly would not have survived O and Muddy. My calculations were wrong, but it did not matter because either way I looked at it the two men would still have died.

As the sun rose I tried to put these thoughts to the back of my mind and concentrate instead on the beauty of the unfolding landscape. Back home in the US nature has been compromised – chemicals poured into the earth and animals so that everything is big and colourless – but in Kenya it is still full. This isn't some kind of romanticised American shit, like the wise old African who speaks in proverbs and parables, but an honest reaction to the fact that I could still see the soil through the grass, that mud ran along even the best of the roads, that I could look at a cow and know that's where my *nyama choma* came from. Life wasn't yet sanitised, it was still as it should be – in tandem with science, but not at the expense of human hands digging into the soil. If I ever came back to Kenya it would be to buy a small farm. Perhaps having found so much ugliness, and having contributed to its creation, I was projecting my hunger for something positive to take back with me on the landscape. A shrink would say that. To which I would say, where's the harm in that?

❝We had been driving for almost twenty-four hours, stopping only for petrol. Finally, about ninety or so kilometres from the border, we came to Butere. The village was very poor, but in contrast to the poverty I had seen in Mathare it was a paradise. There were no UNICEF children running around and the village was meticulously clean – the bare ground still bearing the marks of sisal brooms. Even the bar we walked past maintained a poor dignity.

There was music playing somewhere close by, so we followed it until we came upon a soccer field where a makeshift tent had been erected – it was clear that a wedding was just about to take place. We asked around for Muddy's friend, but no one knew for sure where she was. Even though we were strangers, we were invited to stay for the wedding and we gladly and hungrily agreed.

The wedding ceremony started with a number of smartly dressed little girls and boys walking through the crowd to the makeshift dais, singing a hymn in Kiswahili as they threw handfuls of petals to the ground. They were followed by the wedding party, the groom, dressed in what was clearly a much-worn tuxedo a few sizes too big for him, and finally the bride, dressed in a white gown browned at the edges by the dust. The bride and groom kept looking at each other and breaking into giggles, so much so that the ceremony seemed to be keeping them apart rather than joining them together. The priest was long-winded, but eventually he pronounced them man and wife – though I could only guess, with Muddy too tired to interpret, from the kiss and the clapping.

A reception followed, and after eating a large plate of delicious beef stew with rice I decided to walk around a bit. I hadn't been alone for a long while, and we had been cooped up in the car together for what felt like forever. There really wasn't much to see, but it felt good to just walk around.

On the other side of the soccer field I found an old man trying to hold down a goat for slaughtering. He was surrounded by a group of young men and they were chatting and laughing loudly, but as soon as the old man saw me he called out. I didn't understand a word he said, but it was clear that they needed an extra hand. I went over and held the goat's foreleg as he expertly tilted the animal's head so that it was pressed on the ground, plunged the knife into its throat, and then slit it. The goat tried to kick, but we were firmly holding it to the ground, and I watched indifferently as death slowly overcame it.

The old man started skinning the goat expertly, but when he was almost done he suddenly stopped and handed me the knife, pointing to the final piece of skin that was attached to the carcass. The knife was sharp and it wasn't too difficult to cut away the last of the skin and lift it off the goat – though the young men applauded me like I had just performed some kind of magic trick. Then the old man took my hand and gently guided it so that I disembowelled the goat. I pulled back as soon as the smell from the stomach hit my nostrils – a warm and sticky smell – but laughed when I realised that it wasn't a bad smell. Taking back his knife, the old man then took out the stomach and pointed me to where there was a basin of water. I understood that this was my next job, and taking the stomach from him I went to the basin and started washing out the contents.

Thirty minutes later I returned with the clean stomach and was met by the familiar smell of *nyama choma*. The old man laughed when I showed him the stomach. He gestured until I realised what he was saying – it was too clean and some of the taste would be gone. He walked to the fire, cut a small piece off one of the hunks of roasting meat and, after tossing it back and forth to cool it a little, put it into my hand. It was simply the best piece of food I've ever had.

Soon the meat was ready and it was cut up, put in large bowls and sent off to the wedding party. We, the goat slaughterers, were left with meaty bones, which we gnawed with relish. From somewhere a bottle of vodka was produced and passed around until it was gone. Another appeared, but about halfway into it I left my drunken comrades to go and see what was going on in the tent.

By the time I got back to O and Muddy the chairs in the tent had been moved and a DJ with an old turntable and a collection of vinyl albums was getting ready to do his thing. After a couple of false starts the DJ played a ballad and the bride and groom opened the dance floor. Then he started to play a familiar song – it was Kenny Rogers singing about her believing in him. Muddy tapped me on the shoulder and we walked on to the dance floor with the other couples. O was already dancing drunkenly with an old woman, equally drunk. I had no idea why I wanted to return to the US. Something had been returned to me – though what it was I couldn't be sure. Perhaps it was something as simple as knowing I could be happy again.

Muddy and I started kissing on the dance floor, and as soon as the song was over we walked off and found an empty hut. Not caring whose it was we walked in and made love standing up. Then we returned to the dance floor and, intoxicated with life, continued dancing to the most eclectic collection of songs I've ever heard.

Later, Muddy took to the stage to perform one of her pieces. I didn't understand a word she said because she performed in Kinyarwanda, but I gathered it was about consummation of marriage from the way she moved her hips and how the crowd responded, urging her on and on.

Unfortunately, as soon as she was done with her performance, Muddy decided that she wanted a joint, and encouraged by O she told everyone I needed to rest – after all, I was the drunk American. Her excuse worked and I sullenly followed them to the hut that was pointed out to us as a place I could rest.

I sat on the low bed as O and Muddy rolled their joint, watching the light from the old lantern that lit the hut flicker on the walls. It wasn't long before they were engaged in what they thought was a profound conversation about the meaning of life, enjoying being high. Tired of being around them I decided to take a walk – we would be leaving soon and I needed to walk and 'wash the whiskey out of my blood', as Joshua had put it that night in Madison.

Stepping outside I walked for a while around the outskirts of the village. Then, just as I was thinking of trying to find my way back to the hut the villagers had given us, I caught sight of an electric light. It was a security light – a single bulb – and it was flickering on and off. Intrigued, I walked towards it, only to realise as I approached that the building it was attached to was a little wooden church – it must have been the only building in the village with electricity. I tightened the bulb and in the constant light it suddenly provided I noticed the door to the church wasn't locked. My curiosity got the better of me, and I walked in and turned on the light. Inside, unfinished wooden pews were littered with old Bibles and songbooks, and beside the altar, which had unlit candles all around it, there was huge poster on the wall with the words *WE SHALL NEVER FORGET YOU* printed on it. On closer examination I found that it was surrounded by framed family portraits, small passport photos, with hearts drawn around them, and pictures of smiling babies and lovers holding hands. In the centre hovered a blue-eyed Jesus, looking decidedly out of place, even though this was a church – it reeked of a desperation that contradicted the celebration of life that was still going on outside.

As I turned to leave a large newspaper cutting pasted on cardboard, with a heart drawn around the photograph, caught my eye. I peered into it. The headline read: *Missionaries Caught in Crossfire*. I couldn't quite make out the photograph in the dim light provided by the bulb high in the roof, so I quickly lit one of the candles and held it up to the wall. The photograph was taken in front of a small brick church. Only the parents, a burly white man and his wife, were smiling. The children, three sons and a daughter, dressed in a school uniform, looked like they would rather be somewhere else.

But the girl in the photo – the daughter – I had seen her somewhere before. I felt something tear through my stomach. It was her. It had to be her. It was the white girl! How could it be? Was I going crazy?

My mind flashed back to Maple Bluff, to Joshua's house and the girl's body. 'Wait, wait a goddamn minute,' I said out loud, fumbling for my wallet and taking out her Polaroid. I held it next to this photograph. Her beauty was unmistakable. It shone out even from this old newspaper cutting. I started laughing and yelling. I had found her.

Macy Jane Admanzah. I repeated her name several times, letting it wash over me one syllable at a time. At last I had a name for her. And she hadn't been wearing a cheerleader's uniform when we found her, she was in a school uniform, the same uniform she had on in this photograph. From the cutting, I gathered that the Admanzahs were a missionary family who had been running an underground railroad out of Rwanda during the genocide. The genocidaires had found out and massacred the whole family. Macy Jane survived by pure luck – she was away in boarding school at the time. Her brothers, much younger than her, were not so lucky.

I read the paper as fast as I could. The father and mother were originally from Montana and had first come to Rwanda as teenagers in the 1960s to do their required two years. They fell in love with Rwanda and with each other, and although they returned to the US they felt that their calling was in Africa, in the land of a hill upon a hill. After twenty years they finally had managed to save enough money to come back to Rwanda, and so, cutting all their ties with the US and the Mormon Church, they had returned with their three children in tow as Catholic missionaries, using their savings to buy the land of an old Belgian settler. They had destroyed the mansion and in its place built a modest church which years later would save hundreds of lives.

I ran out of the church, heart racing and almost in tears. Two minutes later I burst into the hut to find Muddy and O still deep in their philosophical discussion. Without saying a word I ran out again and they ran after me, thinking something was wrong. At the church, I showed them the photograph. Muddy rushed out and came back with one of the villagers. But the woman didn't know much – only that she and many others owed the Admanzahs their lives. We asked more of the other Rwandans in the village about the Admanzah family, but no one had any more information beyond their having been killed by the genocidaires. They only came to learn that the family had been killed (including the girl, they had thought) while in a refugee camp, before they found their way to Butere.

'Shit, man, if anyone ever deserved a lucky break it is you,' O said, trying to make sense of the whole thing.

'Luck is the sum of hard work, O,' Muddy corrected him.

They were still high and I left them to go call Mo and update her. She had been looking into the Never Again Foundation, but had found nothing. We agreed that she would hold the big story about the donors, the money laundering and the Refugee Centre until we could substantiate it properly. In the meantime she would begin with the Admanzah story and Joshua's role in the genocide. She did not have to say that he had killed her — we still did not know that for sure — but she had more than enough to be going on with. Mo laughed and told me that her Pulitzer was shaping up well, but I knew that she was also thinking that this story could do both of us in — powerful forces were still at work.

I called the Chief and gave him the news. 'We have a name, at last we have a name,' he said over and over again, as if with the name it was all over.

I understood how he felt. It was a major breakthrough. The name would buy us more time as the media would turn its attention to finding out more about Macy Jane Admanzah.

As I cut the call it suddenly felt as if an arc was closing — I had started off believing Joshua was involved and now I had a confirmed connection. Joshua must have known who the girl was. Why did he withhold her identity? Because without it we had no way of connecting her back to him. Why try to have me killed? Because I had uncovered his past and once what I knew was out in the world his whole life would come crashing down on him.

Macy Jane Admanzah, all along we had been looking for an all-American girl vaguely connected to Africa. This, that her family had been victims of the genocide, we would never have guessed in a million years. But it made sense that she and Joshua would be intimately connected by the genocide. BQ, hadn't BQ said the killer was intimately connected to her? What could be a deeper connection – as pathological as this might sound – than the one shared by a murderer and the grown-up daughter of his victims?

By now I could answer almost all of my questions except one: why would he kill her and yet incriminate himself by leaving her body on his doorstep? Whatever the answer, one thing was for sure, Macy Jane Admanzah never forgot what Joshua had done and she had gone back to the US to get justice, in one form or another. It wasn't over yet, but I was close.

'When in doubt go back to the beginning,' O said when I asked him what he thought. He was high and feeling philosophical, but he was also right, and the beginning was Joshua.

We set out for the border soon afterwards, leaving the whole village in a drunken stupor, save for the little kids. There were no officials at the border post and we drove straight through to the airport where I walked right on to the British Airways flight. We didn't have much of a goodbye, Muddy and I. For now, only solving the case mattered. If I didn't manage it we would all be dead soon enough, killed by assassins for reasons we still did not quite understand.

SMOKESCREENS AND OTHER CRIMES

" I had not changed clothes for days. I stank. Yet I had a big old smile on my face. I could see the horizon – and it looked pretty enough. I proceeded to have a Bud and a meal of rather tasty beef and mashed potatoes, soon after which I promptly fell asleep.

In Chicago I used the one-hour layover to rummage through a pile of newspapers as I enjoyed another Bud. The story was alive and well, though not plastered over the front pages as I had expected. Almost all the papers had new photographs of Macy Jane, with mine as an inset. I had no reason to worry about anyone recognising me, it was an old photo – I was much younger and in uniform – and apart from Homeland Security, who looked over my badge and gun permit and tried half-heartedly to pry some information from me about the case, no one bothered me.

Finally, at about ten or so, I was back on familiar ground – Madison. I took a cab from the airport and asked the driver to let me out four blocks from my apartment, aware that I had to remain cautious. But after walking past my building a couple of times I decided I was being paranoid and made my way up to my stale-smelling apartment. I desperately needed to shower and after letting the water warm up I jumped straight in. Afterwards, wiping the steam off my bathroom mirror, I stared at my face. I had lost weight, my eyes were bloodshot and my beard heavy – I could barely recognise myself. But despite all I had been through I had never felt better in my life. I felt vital.

I put on my best suit – a T-shirt underneath the jacket. I was dressing for destiny. I was going to see Joshua and I was going to rattle him – tell him I knew all about him and Macy Jane and that Macy Jane would have the last word.

Ten minutes later I stepped outside my door. Not again, I thought as my world suddenly went dark.

❮ When I came to I was tied to a chair in my kitchen, a gag tied across my mouth. There was a bright light shining in my face and lying somewhere beneath it I could make out a tray of needles and razors – a clear signal that an unbearable amount of pain was coming my way.

As my eyes adjusted to the light I made out three white men dressed in expensive-looking business suits – exactly like the men who had tried to kill me on my way to Nairobi airport. They were talking amongst themselves, unhurriedly, as if they were in a bar waiting for a beer. The Foundation had me and at any minute Joshua would walk in, I just knew it.

'He's awake,' one of the men said disinterestedly, pulling out his cell to inform someone of the new development.

As we waited the Foundation men continued to chat

amongst themselves. How had they known I was arriving when I did? I wondered. Only four people knew with any certainty which plane I was on. The Chief? Had they gotten to the Chief? But then it struck me that they could have had someone watching Madison airport – it was small enough. Maybe I had simply missed them when I had walked in. It was pointless going on like that, I realised. I was going to die here, and knowing how they had found me wouldn't change anything. I was surprised by how calm I felt. Maybe I had seen too much over the last few days, maybe I had resigned myself to losing my life once too often, but whatever the reason, at that moment I didn't feel my life mattered any more than the ones I had taken.

Then, suddenly, the apartment door opened and an elderly black man entered the room. I had been expecting Joshua, but this frail old man was obviously in charge.

'Are you Ishmael?' he asked almost soothingly as he pulled a chair up beside me.

I nodded.

Immediately he looked over at the men, and without warning two of them grabbed my hands while the third began to push long needles up under my fingernails and into each of my fingers, one finger at a time. I felt my body screaming in pain and I moaned in agony in spite of myself.

'Ishmael, let me explain what is happening here. I have found inflicting pain first establishes trust. I hate the Q and A, you know, I ask you a question, you say you don't know, a little bit of pain, a little bit of truth, et cetera. When I am doing this sort of work I like to clear the ground for truth telling. Do you understand me?'

I couldn't breathe through the gag, but I somehow managed to nod.

'I am also very determined that we conclude our business this evening.' He looked at his watch. 'Or should I say tonight,' he corrected himself. 'Are you in agreement?'

By now sweat was pouring down my face and I was shaking with pain, I felt like I was about to black out, but I managed to nod once again.

The men pulled the needles from my fingers – though it would have been better if they had left them in because it hurt even worse after they had come out. They also removed the gag.

The old man watched as I recovered myself, then reached into his pocket and removed a box of prescription pills. He held it up so that I could read the label – Vicodin. He offered me a pill, but I shook my head. I was going to die on my terms.

'Cancer,' he explained, taking two for himself. 'My time here is not long.'

The way he said it I wasn't sure whether he was referring to time here on earth or in my apartment.

'Do you know who I am?' he continued, sounding as if he was speaking to a nephew he hadn't seen in years.

I shook my head.

'It is okay, Ishmael, you can speak now,' he encouraged.

'No.'

'Well then, let me introduce myself.' He stood up and returned with the logbook Jamal had given me. He flipped through the pages, then put it in front of me and pointed to a name: Andrew Chocbanc. Next to it was a donation of ten thousand Kenyan shillings to the Refugee Centre. I looked up at him in surprise. He was going to kill me for less than two hundred dollars.

'What do you want?' I asked.

He leaned back into his chair and laughed. 'What I want, Ishmael, is the truth. Can you do that? Speak truthfully?' He rattled the tray with the needles. 'When did you arrive?' he asked.

It was a control question – he knew what time I had arrived. 'At about ten pm,' I said.

'And where does the beautiful Muddy live?'

Another control question. I told him. If they could find me, they could find her.

'And your partner, Odhiambo?'

I told him. If Muddy and O were not dead already they soon would be, with or without my help.

'And my good friend, Jamal?'

I said I didn't know.

'Who killed my guitarist?' he asked.

'Muddy, she killed him.'

'You are a sincere man and sincerity should be rewarded,' Chocbanc said, pushing the little table with his instruments away and standing up to wipe my forehead with a cold handkerchief, like a trainer does his boxer, roughly but with affection.

He was giving me a break, trying to get my mind off the questioning. It would make it easier for him to detect a lie. I remained focused.

'These documents,' he finally continued, sitting down again, 'have they been seen by anyone besides the obvious parties?' He held up the logbook and e-mails from Jamal.

I shook my head. Now we were getting to it.

'Now, why don't you name these obvious parties?' he said with a gentle laugh. 'Just to make sure we are on the same page.'

'Me, Jamal, Muddy and Odhiambo. I was taking them in tomorrow morning ... to the Chief,' I said.

'You could have faxed them.'

'Yes, I could, but I didn't.'

'Why?' He pulled the tray closer.

'Trust. I can trust no one,' I answered.

It was the right answer. His world and to a lesser degree mine did not operate on trust. There were no permanent alliances. Suspicion and mistrust made it go round.

'So, if I burn the documents then Africa does not collide with America? What happened in Africa stays in Africa?' he asked.

'Yes.'

Nobody knew about Mo besides me and I would die before I gave her up.

'Your sincerity begs for mine,' Chocbanc offered. 'You are going to die tonight, but I would like you to die at peace with yourself. What would you like to know?'

'Who are you?'

'You, my friend, are threatening a well-balanced money-making machine. You can say I am the Never Again Foundation, but I am legion.' He smiled. 'Behind me are many.'

'So you killed Macy Jane Admanzah?'

'Not me specifically. I am just the invisible partner.

Puppets must have their puppeteers, no?'

The puppets – Joshua, Samuel and Jamal?

'Now, I am afraid we are even,' he said, standing up and straightening his jacket.

'Joshua, it was him … he killed her,' I said in desperation.

'All you need to know is that it was the Foundation,' he said. 'We believe collective work makes for collective success.'

'What happens to Joshua?'

'Balance is about to be restored. We all live happily ever after. Naturally, he lives longer than me … but what the hell!' He said it like he was cracking a joke at a dinner party about a younger colleague.

'Wait, wait … What happens to O and Muddy?' I asked him.

'They die, Ishmael. They die as soon as I make my way over there. Even Jamal, who humours me so. Too greedy for his own good.'

Jamal had been so wrong. The Foundation was everything. The Refugee Centre thought it was in charge, but it was the Foundation that ran everything. Jamal was truly the junior partner. In this maze, he was as lost as I was.

'You don't have to kill them and you know it,' I said, even though I knew it was hopeless.

'Of course I don't … I don't have to do anything. In fact, I could even let you go as long as I destroyed the evidence,' Chocbanc explained patiently. 'But you see, Ishmael, we have to learn from our mistakes. Had Joshua finished what he started years ago we wouldn't be here. The past would be precisely that, the past.'

As he stood to leave Chocbanc looked down at my hands,

then, reaching into his pocket, he produced an expensive-looking pocket watch. I stared at it, unsure of what was happening, until he opened the back of the watch and I saw that it contained a small compartment of cocaine. 'No need to die in pain, Ishmael,' he said as he poured some of it on to my fingers. 'Even we from the underworld, we must say no to cruel and unusual punishments.' He looked around at his men and they nodded in approval.

'My fingernails, I just cleaned them today,' I said out of nowhere, looking down at my bloody hand as my mind flashed back to the fat man in the green suit that O and I had humiliated back in his bar in Nairobi. His tone when he had told us that he had been a boxer had been that of a man speaking of another life. I was not the same man who had cleaned his dirty fingernails less than an hour earlier. That man was alive, vital, looking forward to solving the biggest case of his career.

The men broke out laughing, just as we had at the bartender. Even Chocbanc seemed genuinely amused, smiling at me one last time before he turned and left me to his men.

❝It was simple. I was fucked. Cutting me loose from the chair, the Foundation men bound my hands behind my back. They weren't going to kill me in the apartment. It made sense. They would make it look like I had never made it to my apartment, and with all evidence of what I had uncovered gone and no body, uncertainty would eventually eat the whole thing away. I had no idea where they would take me, but this much I did know: the apartment building was my terrain and I had to make my move soon because once we stepped outside and I was shoved into a car trunk my life was over.

One of the men went ahead to check that the stairwell and parking lot were clear, then, after two or three minutes had passed, the remaining two started to walk me out – one in front and the other behind; their guns drawn. The stairway that spiralled down to the bottom of my apartment building started at my door. I knew that was my only opening. And then I understood that somehow I had been way ahead of myself – it was not without reason that I had mentioned that I had just cleaned my fingernails.

'Watch out for my fingernails, fellas,' I said as they led me to the door.

They broke out laughing again, and in that moment, while they were off their guard, I hurled my whole body against the man leading me out. I couldn't have timed it more perfectly. He had just stepped out of the door and my body weight was enough to throw him into the flimsy rail at the top of the stairs. For a second he hung there, half over the rail, scrambling to get his footing, and then it broke. Stumbling forward, I would have followed him screaming into the abyss, but the guy behind me instinctively pulled me back. Using that momentum I pushed him hard against the door frame, knocking the wind out of him. Then I ran for dear life, all the while trying to undo my hands.

By the time the rope gave in and my hands were free I was on the second floor. Always do the unexpected. That's what I had learned from O. The motherfucker upstairs would expect me to run for the door and out into the street looking for help, but instead I gently pulled a fire axe from the wall and waited for him to come down the stairs. I waited until the moment he was about to see me then I let him have it. He hadn't hit the ground before I had his gun in my hand.

Rushing outside I found Chocbanc and the other Foundation man in the parking lot. I shot the Foundation man first, twice. As he slumped to the ground, Chocbanc raised his hands and started to try to talk me down.

'Tell me something I don't know,' I yelled at him.

He hesitated and I waited for two or three seconds, knowing that he had told me all he knew – confessed all his sins to a dying man.

'I killed the girl,' he said.

He started to say something else, but I shot him once in the head. All I needed now was Joshua, and I was going to go after him, nothing else mattered.

❝ In Maple Bluff I rang Joshua's doorbell, feeling like destiny itself. Despite the fact that it was close to three am he opened it moments later. Just like the first time I had met him he was fully dressed – suit, shoes and everything – and even stranger than this was the wide smile that was plastered across his face, it was as if I was a friend he had been expecting for a long time.

Joshua led me to the spacious kitchen at the back of the house where he proceeded to open a bottle of wine, pouring two glasses and offering me one of them. A week earlier, when it had still been fun and games, I would have been happy enough, but there was no way I was going to drink his wine, especially when he himself had poured it.

'I see Ishmael quickly learn terrible ways of my people … Mistrust even when one means no harm,' he said, moving to the fridge and coming back with two Tuskers, one of which he opened and placed on the table in front of me.

I didn't say anything. Instead I lifted the Tusker to my lips and took a gulp – it tasted good and for a second I was back in Africa, at The Hilton Hotel bar, getting drunk with O.

'I have a question for you, Joshua,' I finally said, taking out the gun I had taken from the Foundation man back at my apartment block. 'Do you want to die tonight?'

He didn't seem startled. In fact, it was as if he hadn't heard what I had said.

I unscrewed the silencer and placed it on the table, well within my reach. 'In that case, let's talk,' I said.

His face was hard, but I knew he wanted to talk, he wouldn't have opened the door if it were otherwise.

'You think you know, but you don't know,' he finally said. 'Yes, I wanted you killed for what you know about me. But you also my friend, even in Africa you remain my friend.'

I simply stared back at him. I knew what he was thinking, if only he could get past me or convince me of his innocence he would be home free. 'What do you mean?' I eventually asked him.

He sighed tiredly. 'The Foundation … very powerful. I am pawn in the chess set. They make me hero, okay? I make them money and they pay me. A good relationship only … only they decide to get rid of me because of that girl. And what better way than to use her against me? Then you become my friend.' He paused to study my face. 'When the Foundation come after me,' he explained, 'enemy of my enemy become friend.'

I smiled at him and took another swig of Tusker.

'All the other things they say I did, yes I did,' Joshua continued, trying desperately to explain himself. 'Yes, I hated them. But now I grow. I go to Kenya and see Kikuyu and Luo live together. I come to America and see black and white live together. I grow. But what I know then? Look, Ishmael, life was simple. I teach them, I live with them, but what they do for me? They take best jobs, fuck my women and take my best land ...'

'I don't care about all that other shit,' I said, interrupting him. 'I only care about Macy Jane Admanzah.'

'Macy, I did not touch. Her family, fucking missionaries ... Her family, I order kill. Ten years later she is in my doorway ... dead. The Foundation want me out of image. She go to them, looking for me, they panic and decide to get rid of me and her both. They bring her here and kill her. Money ... all about the money.'

It took Joshua almost an hour to explain everything. The Admanzahs, as I knew, had been missionaries in Rwanda. According to him they were racists who had been running an underground railroad for those escaping genocide – 'They treat them like little children,' he told me, 'even old men and women.' He hadn't known that their church was an underground railroad until some of the people he had helped had told him about it, suggesting that if they joined hands they could save many more lives. Joshua was of course using the school as a cover to lure more innocents out of hiding and he wasn't keen on competition, so he had ordered fifteen or so of his killers to descend on the Admanzah family – killing them all, or so he had thought.

After the genocide everything was so confused that no one had come forward to accuse Joshua of killing the Admanzahs or of using his school as a false beacon. And in Kenya he was welcomed as a hero by those he had actually helped to escape the genocide – they had no idea that he had saved them only to lure more people to their deaths. Then the Never Again Foundation had arrived on the scene and Samuel Alexander had found out about Joshua and recruited him to be their poster boy. When Samuel had found out the truth Joshua didn't say, but he must have known by the time Mary Karuhimbi and the Kokomat women came to him. By then of course the conscience of the world was bleeding millions of dollars into the Foundation and Samuel had the finances to pay them off. Luckily, they had jumped at the money and Joshua's secret had remained just that.

In fact, everything had gone well again until an of-age Macy Jane Admanzah had decided to seek justice for her family and expose Joshua for what he really was. Naturally her first port of call had been the Refugee Centre in Nairobi, and it was there that Samuel Alexander had told her that Joshua was now based in the United States. Joshua then claimed that Samuel had paid for Macy Jane's ticket to the US, telling her that he wanted to help her confront Joshua and expose him, even promising to help take him to the International Criminal Court.

What Samuel had discovered, Joshua claimed, was that he could do two things at the same time – get rid of Joshua, who was costing the Foundation quite a bit of money, and get rid of Macy Jane by killing her and tying the murder to Joshua.

Of course this would mean the end of the Foundation, but it wouldn't take Samuel long to find another golden boy and set up a new foundation as long as he still had control of the Refugee Centre. Joshua only figured this out later. He had no idea his world was about to collapse until he came home and found Macy Jane dead on his porch. I knew Samuel had been scheming money from his partners and that the Refugee Centre and the Foundation were in financial trouble, two more reasons for getting rid of Joshua and starting over.

Why had Samuel Alexander committed suicide?

He was a weak man, Joshua replied with contempt. He didn't have the stomach for what he had created, especially after he had ordered Macy Jane Admanzah's murder and instead of Joshua taking the fall I had flown to Nairobi to look for answers. Again this made sense to me. The suicide note was addressed to Joshua – something Joshua could not have known. Samuel was apologising to Joshua for destroying what they had created together.

Why couldn't Joshua, once incriminated, become a whistle-blower?

I knew the answers even before he gave them. His life. He would not have lived to tell his story. And his past. He had thought he could still protect his secret.

'But why not get rid of the body? Why leave it where you found it?' I asked him.

When he came home and found her there he had had to think fast. From the state of her body he could tell that she hadn't been dead for long and he knew that whoever had left her body would call the police as soon as they were in the clear. In the space of a few minutes he had found her purse, gone through her pockets and removed the African jewellery she had been wearing. He had then put everything into a plastic bag and stuffed it into his bedroom toilet. Finally, he had called the police.

I picked up my cellphone and called the station to find out if he was telling the truth about the calls. For a detective, a suspect's guilt or innocence can lie in a single detail. Sometimes it is simply the kind of detail that the suspect would have no knowledge of unless they had been in a certain place at a certain time that somehow validates his or her side of the story. Sometimes it is something that somehow resolves a contradiction or answers a question that has undermined all possible theories. For Joshua the question had always been why he would leave the body outside his own door when he would have had time to dispose of it if he had wanted to – no one would have traced Macy Jane to him had we found her in some dumpster somewhere.

A few minutes later my cell rang. Joshua wasn't lying about the calls – there were two: one from his cellphone and another from a phone booth just outside Maple Bluff. The cop on duty played me both calls. The first caller was clearly an American, most probably a Caucasian male. He told the operator that he had just witnessed a murder and he gave Joshua's address, before hanging up. The other call, just two minutes later, was from Joshua. He was reporting finding a dead girl on his porch. The operator asked him to take the girl's pulse and make sure she was still breathing, but Joshua was way ahead of him. 'No, I try bring her back,' he said, 'but she dead.'

The more I thought about what Joshua was telling me

the more sense it made. He knew he was being set up and that the killer would have called the cops, so he knew that he did not have enough time to get rid of the body. All he could do was strip it of anything that could help us identify Macy Jane. With his past safely hidden in Africa, he had been sure he could outrun it. He had not counted on my being sent to Kenya.

The two calls were a small detail that had gotten lost early on in what had been a chaotic and sensational case. There were still a lot more questions to be answered but Joshua's story explained who had killed Macy Jane Admanzah and why. It also explained why I had thought he was guilty of something right from the beginning – he had been trying to hide something from me, but it was his past. He was guilty of many terrible things, but at that moment I was sure that he had not killed Macy Jane Admanzah.

Finishing my Tusker, I picked up my piece and stood to take my leave of the man that only an hour earlier I had been ready to kill. What was going to happen to Joshua? Were we going to punish him for a crime he did not commit? Would we let him go free despite his role in the genocide? Maybe there would be enough evidence to bring him to trial for crimes against humanity. I didn't know. There were the Kokomat women, and there would surely be others. I wanted to talk it over with the Chief, file my report and let the powers that be decide.

'Ishmael, I am bad man,' Joshua said as I moved towards the door. 'I know, you know. I do unspeakable things. But, Ishmael, I do not kill that girl.'

Suddenly I wondered why his being innocent of Macy

Jane Admanzah's murder was so important to him. He surely knew his past was about to be revealed and that his life would be destroyed once people knew what he had really done during the genocide.

'I do not know, Ishmael,' he said sadly when I asked him about it. 'Maybe I change. Maybe I change, and I desire truth be known.'

As I drove back to my apartment complex, where I knew I would find the Chief, I couldn't help thinking about the Admanzahs. For some people they were racists. For others they were true Christians. Some would think of them as bleeding-heart liberals. While others would say that they were simply misguided. But here is a question for you: what makes a husband and wife uproot their family from the US, from a farm that is doing well, from a school a bit conservative but nevertheless a school that offers hope to their children, and take them to Africa?

I had seen many Admanzahs in Allied Drive. In Allied Drive white folk were always trying to save black folk, trying to get them off drugs and out of gangs. Forget the white trash and the rednecks; well-to-do white people wanted to save black folk. So perhaps the Admanzahs enjoyed playing Jesus to Africans. But did they deserve to die for it? What life had they taken? On the contrary, they had saved lives.

When I finally made it to the Chief he was predictably furious – the violence had come to America, to a small town called Madison in Wisconsin, and he had four bodies to deal with, three of them white.

'Have you gone crazy? You have opened us up wide to get fucked,' he yelled as he dragged me out of the car. 'You are coming with me to the station right now.'

'Am I under arrest?'

'How the fuck am I supposed to know?' he asked as he pushed me into his car. 'I know nothing ... '

Back at the station I explained everything as best I could. The Chief had calmed down during the drive and by the time I had finished my story he looked almost happy. We finally had the answers we had been looking for.

'We have Macy Jane's killers, it looks like, but Joshua, he gets away with everything?' the Chief said. It was more of a statement than a question. 'Feed the story to the dogs,' he instructed.

That was exactly what I had planned to do. I checked into a motel, called Mo and updated her. For the first time since I'd known her she offered to come over and make sure I was okay, but I told her I was fine. I drifted off with the receiver still in my hand, thoughts of Muddy swimming through my mind.

LET THE DEAD BURY THE DEAD

« Mo's story broke later that morning in *The Madison Times* – and it broke huge. By now she had developed good relationships with several big-time papers and TV stations and they all wanted a piece of the story. It was sweeter than a Mafia bust; a new sort of crime with the good and bad guys in disguise – there was the shadowy Chocbanc, now dead; there was the Macy Jane Admanzah angle; Joshua's story; the Foundation, its board and the CEOs; there was even my story. So, within hours, headline after headline screamed *Justice for Macy Jane Admanzah At Last*, *Beauty and the Beasts*, *Sex and Violence on the Dark Continent*, *The Black Prince* (not sure if that was me or Joshua), et cetera. Even the KKK circulated leaflets congratulating the Chief and me, saying we were a good example of what our race could offer if it applied itself.

That evening I called BQ and asked him to meet me for a beer. I had never done this before, but after a moment's hesitation he agreed. I wanted to tell him the case was finally over, that justice had been done by Macy Jane Admanzah. I wanted to tell him because I had never forgotten his off-hand comment that someone who knew her well, who might have even loved her, had committed the murder.

We sat around for a few hours, talking about the case, Northern and Southern women and even country music. I now had encyclopaedic knowledge of Kenny Rogers – turns out he is not well liked in the South – a sell-out of sorts. It was great to sit around in no particular hurry, drinking beer and listening to music. We played darts and pool – he won easily; my fingers, even though not painful, were still cumbersome.

'Looky here, my friend,' he finally said, drunkenly sucking on an unlit cigarette. 'We sure are friends now, Ishmael, ain't we?' He leaned closer to me and placed his hand on my shoulder.

'Sure, BQ,' I answered. 'We are friends.' I meant it too.

'Well then, my friend, your case. It raises more questions than a hog at a Christmas party.'

'What do you mean?' I asked him.

'It's too complicated … just too damn complicated,' he answered. 'And, my friend, murders are always simple as rain. You know that.'

From my angle everything fitted. Yes, it was a complicated chain of events, but Joshua had reconstructed the motives behind the crime for me and it made sense. But it was BQ saying this – not the Chief, Muddy, O, or even Mo (they were all too close to the case and all had a vested interest in the outcome for one reason or another). He was as dispassionate as anyone could get – his work, cutting up bodies and holding back his anger long enough to find the cause of death, told me that I should take what he was telling me seriously.

'What do you mean?' I asked him.

'Looky here, my friend,' BQ drawled. 'You are asking me to believe that Macy Jane Admanzah came here to expose Joshua, and that whoever it is that was controlling the Never Again Foundation, Chocbanc or whoever, decides to get rid of Joshua before he brings all of the whole thing crashing down around him? So they kill Macy Jane Admanzah and leave her body by his door?'

'Can you just tell me where this is going?' I asked.

'I have no idea, but even this drunken fool knows this: a person cannot be guilty of genocide and innocent of murder. It just doesn't add up. His instinct is to kill, just like a scorpion stings.'

I thought back to the statement he had made in the morgue as we had stood over Macy Jane Admanzah's body little more than a week earlier – 'My guess is it was someone who knew her well, someone who might even have loved her ... ' I asked him about it, but he couldn't remember saying it. I was relieved – he had nothing but a hunch.

'So, Ishmael, we still friends?' BQ asked after a few minutes of silence.

'Yeah, of course, man, we're still friends,' I answered and laughed.

And that was that. We sat around drinking beer and singing along to country music until the bar closed. I got home feeling neither depressed nor happy, just drunk.

❰ I woke the following day to find that there had been two immediate casualties from Mo's story. The first casualty was the Never Again Foundation itself. The board had resigned

175

even as the powers that be had moved to investigate them for fraud and racketeering. And it wasn't only the board. Politicians in the US, Rwanda and Kenya whose names appeared in the logbook were also forced to resign, such was the outrage. The US Senate even went as far as to set up a commission to investigate not just the Never Again Foundation but also all major charitable organisations. The second casualty was Joshua Hakizimana. The world's rage was focused on Joshua. Not for the genocide, but for making the world believe in him. It was as if it had been discovered that Mandela was actually a prison guard. In the days that followed Maple Bluff was mobbed with people literally crying for a piece of him, Hollywood stars tore his picture on live TV and the ICC launched its own investigation into his role in the genocide.

It seemed to me that everything was going to turn out right. However, as the weeks rolled into months the stories about the board and the trials got smaller and smaller until nothing more was heard about them. And as for Joshua, well it wasn't long before the Johnnie Cochran type lawyers came crawling out of the woodwork – he was an American citizen after all and there was due process. Later it became apparent that he couldn't be tried for genocide in the US, only for money laundering and the lesser crime of tampering with evidence. But even on these charges everything was not as straightforward as you might think. Joshua had covered his tracks well and the FBI found only one bank account with about two million dollars in it. He couldn't account for some of it, but he made a lot on his speaking tours, and if you factored in his professor's salary the discrepancy wasn't as much as you might think. And later that same month the ICC found it had no credible witnesses. The Kokomat women were compromised, and no one could say for sure that Joshua had ordered the murder of the Admanzah family. Even my testimony was questioned in light of evidence that I had 'engaged in extra-judicial killings' in Kenya. And his confession, told to a detective 'who had just been tortured and killed four men', was 'agitated' and 'without a warrant', was inadmissible.

The world never fully lets go of its heroes and slowly Joshua was rehabilitated. Even Mo couldn't stop the tide as slowly students and professors came to his defence – claiming that there was no evidence of his involvement in the genocide. Finally, sensing the turning of the tide, the Madison black community weighed in, speaking of Joshua's contributions to their development programmes.

Three months later Macy Jane Admanzah was all but forgotten and Joshua was back teaching his classes. What I hated most were the cops who patted me on the back saying, 'You can't win them all.' I had a front row seat to a genocidaire getting away with it. It wasn't a question of winning, it was about recouping a sense of justice.

But so it was. The Chief was promoted to Police Commissioner and I to Chief Detective. Everyone except the dead came off better.

❰ While all this was happening I volunteered to accompany Macy Jane Admanzah's body back to Rwanda. Although I hadn't known her I still felt like she was a family member who had made a contribution to my life for which I could never repay her – taking her back to Rwanda was the least I could do.

In Kigali the airport was crawling with media – even the ragtag *Madison Times* had sent Mo over to cover the whole thing. This was the closest a non-Rwandan had come to a state funeral, something confirmed by the fact that it was the President who came to meet the body at the airport. I chatted with the tall thin man for a few minutes. He had been the commander of the rebels and had heard the rumour of a headmaster using his school to lure people to their deaths, but at the time it had felt like a myth. 'Even in evil times, there is a greater evil we do not allow ourselves to imagine,' he explained.

We took a few photographs together before he draped the coffin with a Rwandan flag. Then, strangely enough, we spoke about guns and he explained why to this day he prefers an AK-47 – light, economical and easy to use. I suppose guns and death were the only things we had in common. Finally, he thanked me and was whisked away by the secret police.

Later, I was driven through the city, part of a slow funeral procession that was met by street after street lined with school children and their parents. I couldn't help but wonder what it was about Macy Jane Admanzah that drew them to her. Was it her whiteness? Was it that she was a foreigner who had lost everything just like them? Or was it simply that she was a representation of all that was wrong with the world – another young person who had lost her life to the genocide? I didn't know.

Finally, we came to a majestic Catholic church. They had

flown in a father from France and everything else followed suit – over the top. Would this simple family of missionaries have wanted this kind of a funeral for their daughter? But then she, and they by extension, had been adopted by the state, and this was all about what the state wanted – politician after politician took to the stage, condemning genocide and applauding the Admanzahs.

It was only when I had been out buying the clothes she would be buried in, at a Madison store called Betty Bling, that I had begun to wonder about Macy Jane's extended family. Her relatives were probably still in Montana, but no one had contacted us, leading me to believe that the Admanzah family had been excommunicated after they had converted to Catholicism.

Outside Betty Bling, on State Street, hundreds of college students had been going about their lives – drinking coffee, holding hands, playing guitars and doing quick paintings for change. But Macy Jane's life was over and that afternoon I had felt the loss of her in ways I would probably never be able to explain. I had stood in the shop for a long time, as sales clerk after sales clerk had come up to ask me if I needed help. Finally, exasperated, I had asked one of them what she would like to be buried in. The shock on her face had jerked me back to reality and I had rushed to explain what I was doing there. Luckily, she had recognised me when I had walked in, and once my explanation was complete she had relaxed and introduced herself. Her name was Betty – the owner of the store.

Betty was about Macy Jane's height and build. We went through several outfits, her trying each one of them on – a strange thing to do, I had realised later, but it had worked. Finally, we had settled on a white shirt, a red blazer and a long black skirt, complemented by a pearl necklace and a simple copper-wire bracelet.

'No charge. You did a good thing ... It's the least I can do,' Betty had said nonchalantly when it had come time to pay. And somehow those words had finally broken me and I had started crying. I had never felt that torn before – not just angry and sad, but as if I was being pulled apart piece by piece.

Betty had helped me to a fitting room where I had sat for a while trying to pull myself together. Eventually, I had composed myself and left with my bundle of clothes and a splitting headache.

Finally the church service ground to a halt and we accompanied Macy Jane to her final resting place: Heroes' Acre. This was where those who had been of great service to the country were buried. I was asked to say a few words and although I had known that this moment was coming I hadn't prepared – I couldn't think of anything to say, much less how to say it.

'I don't have much to say except that I am touched by the love you have shown Macy Jane Admanzah in death,' I started. 'Hers was a lonely anonymous death. I hope we can make it count for something.'

I knew I was expected to say more, but I had said all I needed to. Then I remembered a Langston Hughes poem that we had memorised in elementary school: 'What happens to a dream deferred?' I started. 'Does it dry up, like a raisin in the sun? Or fester like a sore, and then run? Does it stink like rotten meat? Or crust and sugar over, like a syrupy sweet? Maybe it just sags, like a heavy load. Or does it explode?'

I paused, trying to think of a way to end. I was no Muddy with words and there was no shame in that.

'What happens to justice deferred? What happens to love deferred?'

I finished and left the podium to silence.

Finally, she was put into the ground and it was over.

❝ Muddy and O had come to the funeral but it wasn't until after the service that we were able to meet. Even though it was only a few weeks since I had last seen them, they both looked younger than I remembered – Muddy with her dreadlocks pulled back, wearing a simple white-and-blue dress, her skin shiny from the heat, and O dressed in a white T-shirt and stiff blue jeans. With the weight of the case gone, they were doing well.

I held on to Muddy for a long time, but just when I thought I was going to break down and cry O tapped me on the shoulder and suggested that we go for a beer. We went to the Planet Club, where among the drunken tourists we felt like the foreigners. After a lot of beer Muddy and O bummed a joint from one of the waiters and like high-school kids we hid behind the hotel and smoked it. I probably shouldn't have joined them because I slipped into senseless laughter for the better half of the night.

In the morning we left O in his room and started the drive to Muddy's village in a rented jeep. A few minutes from the city the country opened up to rolling hills. It was hard to imagine that just a few years earlier this land had been soaked in blood as neighbour gave up neighbour, friends became foes and whole families were hacked to death.

Once, when in college, my ex-wife and I had gone to see a civil war re-enactment at Gettysburg. I do not remember what possessed us to go, but we did – spending the whole afternoon watching hundreds of volunteers dressed in Northern and Southern uniforms duke it out. The whole thing looked silly – even the bearded fellow who read Lincoln's Gettysburg address. It was too clean, the grass in the field where the original battle had taken place too green, and the soldiers too chubby. But we were determined, and we watched the whole thing despite feeling awkward – there were only a handful of black people in the audience. As we drove to Muddy's village, up and down hills and valleys dotted with banana trees, I couldn't help but wonder whether a few hundred years from now the genocide would be re-enacted in just the same way to open-mouthed children and teenagers.

Muddy was driving and she did not say much. With her eyes hidden behind dark glasses I couldn't tell what she was thinking. This was her first time back in the country of her birth, and the irony that she had returned to bury a white woman must have been apparent to her.

We drove on, eating up mile after mile until we passed large metal gates with the name Joshua Hakizimana High School written in a huge metal frame hanging above them. A little further down the straight asphalt road that ran from the gate a huge flag with Joshua's face swung in the wind. We stopped and marvelled. They had renamed the school after Joshua, Muddy explained needlessly. I suggested we go in, but Muddy had seen enough and we drove on.

An hour or so later we saw a small wooden church on top of a hill. It had been freshly painted a blinding white.

'This is the church,' Muddy said absent-mindedly.

This church, now restored, had belonged to the Admanzahs. There were a number of cars – belonging to tourists and reporters – parked outside, but instead of making our way inside we walked through the graveyard until we found what we were looking for – their graves. It was easy to tell that they had been hastily tidied up – fresh cement work, repainted headstones and a new white picket fence around each of them gave the game away.

'Why didn't they bury Macy here?' I asked Muddy.

'Not as dramatic as Heroes' Acre,' she promptly answered.

We went into the church and found a group of about fifteen or so reporters listening to a guide. He was explaining, in English (for the benefit of American journalists), about the rows upon rows of skulls that lined the walls. They probably ran into the hundreds, all cleaned and sparkling white, looking back at us in silent accusation.

I couldn't take it and rushed outside, but as I was throwing up I felt a hand on my shoulder. It was Mo. She was close to tears, and for a moment we stayed like that – me leaning over heaving and her with her hand on my shoulder, shaking her head from side to side. She was a tough reporter but this was too much even for her.

A little while later Muddy came outside and I introduced her to Mo, breaking the spell grief had thrown over us. We found a little bench outside and sat there for a few minutes, talking about nothing until we were well enough to part ways.

Muddy and I left the church and travelled on to her village. When we got there we found a group of people sitting under a tree, a few elderly-looking folk sitting at a table and a man standing all alone to the left of the group. The man was saying something, and as we climbed out of the car I asked Muddy what was going on. Accused of murder, he was defending himself, she explained. He was saying that it wasn't him that the witnesses were describing. I wanted to stand around and watch – this was a traditional court – but Muddy said it made her sick to look at the man and hurried me on.

As we walked away, a few people turned to look at us, but it was obvious that they didn't recognise Muddy. Practically her whole village had been wiped out, Muddy told me as we walked. These people were resettled refugees, and with them had come some of their killers. After the killing ended where were they to go, if not back to their communities and hope no one remembered? But people remembered and that was why that young man was on trial.

We made it to a run-down brick house. There were several children in the compound and some women looking after them. Muddy asked if we could come in, and the women agreed. Once inside Muddy asked the women if she could look around. They asked her why and she explained.

'We thought no one had survived,' they said as they hugged Muddy joyfully – strangers turned into family by death and violence. 'This is your home,' they said to her, or at least I think that is what they were saying to Muddy from the gestures they were making. But she simply shook her head and smiled.

Walking around to the back of the house we found three

graves marked with wooden headstones, the names of the dead carefully burnt into them. There were rose bushes growing on the mounds of soil, each one of them surrounded by a ring of carnations – the families that lived in the house had obviously been taking care of the graves.

Muddy was visibly moved. Thinking she wanted to be alone, I started to walk away, but she reached for my hand and slid it around her waist. 'Stay,' she said. So I did, holding her in silence as she sobbed away quietly.

'A word is flesh,' she began to repeat to herself over and over again. 'A word is flesh.' And then she would say their names over and over again. 'A word is life. A word is flesh.'

Even though she was not raising her voice, her chant became louder and louder until I was lost in it. I found that I was breathing heavily and I felt myself getting light-headed – it was as though I was going to have a panic attack. And then, just as suddenly as she had started, Muddy stopped and we stood together in silence.

When she was ready, we walked back into the compound and she gave the women her contacts. They hugged and then we left for Kigali.

It was evening by the time we got back to the hotel and we were pleasantly surprised to find O and Mo chatting away, the table in front of them crowded with empty beer bottles. We sat around and told stories and jokes. A DJ started playing and we danced, or closer to the truth, stormed the dance floor. Later that night, Muddy and I, alone at last, made love, and the following morning we travelled to the airport together before finally parting ways. Everything had come to an end. Everyone had some sense of closure.

THE AFRICAN CONNECTION

❝ There are things we all do that regardless of how bad we feel always make us feel better. For some it's cooking, for others it's sex, but for me it's running – it's the closest I come to meditation. By the time I got home from Rwanda I hadn't run for close to two months and I was beginning to feel like my body was clamping up. It was time – the case was behind me, I was due back at work soon and I was feeling ready to regain my life.

Stepping out of my apartment building, the sun streaming into my eyes, I took a deep breath of the crisp fall air and decided to run my usual circuit, past the graveyard where I always enjoyed watching names roll by. I knew this was going to be a good run when by the end of the first mile my breathing – which had started out a little heavy – was steady and my feet were moving in a good rhythm. I could just enjoy moving. I could listen to myself – my breathing, the sound of my feet hitting the ground and my heart thumping against my ribs – and know that I was alive. But somewhere around the third mile I hit the wall. Any runner can tell you about the wall – the mind tells the body to stop and the body begins to believe the mind, exhaustion sets in, breathing becomes short gasps, muscles burn and pure agony seems only a few steps away. But if you can get past the wall the mind lets the body go, and this, for me, was the prize – why I ran. As my body took control of itself my mind was washed by thoughts and ideas that came over me without my willing them.

As my mind let my body go, it wandered to Muddy: I saw her as I had first seen her on stage, then as she had appeared at our last meeting; how sad she had seemed even while appearing to be happy. Then I was back at the graveyard, looking at the names as I passed them, reading them aloud, one after the other. Then it was off to Macy Jane Admanzah's funeral. Was she finally at peace? How could she be if her family's killer was free?

As I ran on little pieces of the case began to flow into my mind at a steady pace, each piece fitting snugly into the next. Then some of the lessons I had learned with O in Kenya began to surface: nothing is random; look at who wins, who comes out on top. And there was only one big winner, and that was Joshua. With everyone else dead, the Foundation in one form or another was his to inherit. Only Jamal stood in his way and he would be no match for Joshua. And more than this, his tarnished reputation had been restored – he had become a victim all over again. His past had been exposed and the claims against him thrown out of court. It was as if he had been forgiven for his role in the genocide. No one would ever again be able to question his heroism. His biggest gain was his freedom from his past.

Then I decided to ask the toughest question of all the other way round. What would Joshua have gained by murdering

Macy Jane Admanzah and leaving her body on his doorstep?

There was only one answer that made any sense. He had let the finger of suspicion point at him initially because he knew the search for Macy Jane's identity would eventually point to others. No matter how suspicious it all looked he had known from the beginning that he would never be found guilty, not without an answer to the question of why he would kill her and then leave her body outside his own door. And indeed, when I had finally found out Macy Jane Admanzah's identity, I had cast doubt on my own suspicions by asking myself that very same question. He knew his plan didn't have to go perfectly – only a few things had to work right and everything else would be a bonus. He simply had to eliminate those associated with the Foundation in a way that would leave him still standing, no matter how wounded. The media, the public and the police would do the rest for him. He had outwitted his enemies. It was him. It had to be him.

I created another scenario in my head as I ran. Macy Jane Admanzah had gone to the Never Again Foundation to blow the whistle on Joshua. Perhaps Samuel Alexander had sent her to the US. Perhaps she had come on her own. Either way it made sense that the Foundation and Joshua would work together as one to contain a mutual threat. And with Macy Jane gone, balance, as Chocbanc had called it, would have been restored. But somewhere along the way plans changed. Why did they change?

According to Joshua and Jamal, greed was the culprit. Even for Chocbanc greed had been involved, but whose greed? Who stood poised to inherit the earth? It was Joshua – he had seen an opportunity and had taken it. He had killed Macy

Jane Admanzah, cleaned her up and left her on his doorstep.

And then there was BQ telling me that the murder was personal. He was Macy Jane's killer. It was the only way the case made sense. I had to confront him. I still had nothing beyond a theory, but if I could get him to speak I was sure he would supply all the answers – now that he had fooled everyone, and was in the clear, he would be willing to talk; it would be in character.

I thought of rushing back to my apartment, taking a shower, changing into a T-shirt, jeans and sneakers and then driving to his house. But I was close to Maple Bluff and I would look more convincing, harmless even, if I ran all the way to his house. I got into an easy pace. It was going to be one hell of a walk back.

❮ Joshua – dressed in jeans, a black shirt and light leather shoes – was clearly surprised to see me, but he quickly recovered and invited me in. He was packing, he said, leaving later that night for Rwanda and Kenya for a while. It was time he confronted his past. But I knew he was going to try and rebuild an empire.

In spite of the early hour he produced a bottle of wine and poured two glasses. 'In the morning I eat wine; in the evening I consume breakfast,' he said with a laugh.

'Can I have a glass of water?' I asked. I was hot and sweaty after my run and the last thing I felt like was a glass of wine.

'Wine no turn to water for you?' He laughed as he went to the kitchen and came back with a glass of water.

I gulped the water down, knowing that the gesture would

open him up – for people like us a gesture would always establish trust faster than a word.

'So, Ishmael, what do you want?' he asked.

I told him that I knew, that I had figured it all out. 'Tell me everything, Joshua,' I said. 'Surely you must want at least one person to know.'

'Why?' he asked, although he was clearly interested.

'Because you've won. Look, you got away with the genocide, didn't you? Who better to know the truth than I?' I asked him.

It made a kind of crazy sense. There is no sweeter victory than one in which you tell your beaten opponent how you defeated him or her.

'You have point there ... ' he started. 'Okay, Ishmael. But we make rules to make game interesting, eh?' he said with a look of pure glee in his eyes.

'Sounds like a plan,' I said as I picked up my glass of wine.

'Let's see ... Simple rule. You ask one question only. I answer, make one statement only, then we finish. Okay? You agree?' He made it sound like we were little kids making up ground rules for some game.

I agreed. I needed to know only one thing with certainty. Everything else – the hows and the whys, the moralisations and justifications – came a distant second.

'Did you kill her?' I asked.

He took a deep breath. 'Yes, I kill the girl,' he answered without a flicker of emotion. 'She come to me, so I take opportunity for myself and kill her. She dress like that because she know I like young women, and she want to seduce me then give me heroin ... She look for justice for herself. But she didn't know I know about her ... So, we go for a ride to the lake in car I rent, and she start her move to seduce me. I play for a bit, then I tell her we come back to my place. I leave her in room and go meet friends for drink, then I come back. She want to continue. I play more, then I turn her face on bed and I push down till she die. Then I put her in warm water. I drive car to bar, to return to rental place tomorrow and pick up my car where I leave it. I come back quickly, dry her hair, put her on the stairs and inject her with heroin for final effect. Then I call police. I shower and change, but forget to add socks ... '

Everything had fallen in place. When she saw that the Never Again Foundation was just stringing her along Macy Jane Admanzah must have understood that she didn't have enough evidence, power and money to buy justice, so she had decided to get it herself. And when she had turned up on his doorstep Joshua had seen his opportunity and killed her.

'Why didn't you just let her go? She had no evidence against you ... No one would have investigated her claims,' I asked angrily, knowing that now he had finally told me the truth Joshua wouldn't be able to resist breaking his own rules and telling me everything.

'I tell you when you come to my house before,' Joshua said. 'That part truth. Samuel want to eliminate me by sending her to the Foundation. Foundation want her gone, I want her dead too, but Samuel and Foundation think they get rid of me by killing the girl and plant evidence to say it was I. So I kill her first. Death for her inescapable, from me, Samuel or Foundation.'

'How did you know they wanted to implicate you in her murder?'

'I get told … Too much greed in Foundation, people compete and secrets leak out. And Samuel behave like stranger, so I suspect as well. I mean, how you suspect me now? Many things, some without name, no?'

'And people like Jamal, where do they fit in?'

'Jamal small man who think he big. Three principals: Chocbanc, whom you kill, Samuel, who kill himself, and I. And now only I remain,' he said proudly.

'If all that you say is true, why did Chocbanc try to kill me and not you?'

'Ishmael, you surprise me. Very simple. No you, no evidence to point at him or Foundation or I. No victor between him and I. No victor and it just me and Chocbanc making money. He want things return normal. He was old man, you know?'

I had to laugh at the pained look on his face. The stubbornness of old folk, his expression seemed to say, so stuck in their ways.

'What about the first call to the police? Who made the call?'

He laughed. I knew the answer already.

'Money talks, eh? The same person from Foundation who tell me plot, I pay him.' He paused, studying me intently. 'I think you have all answer now,' he finally said. 'I do good and answer four or so question. I think you leave now.' He was suddenly very aware of himself – as if something had broken a spell and he had returned to the real world. 'Okay, we conclude our business. Everyone happy, no?'

'No, our business is not yet concluded,' I replied as he stood up to show me out. 'I do have one last thing to say …'

'Of course, Detective, always one last thing, no?'

'I promised Macy Jane Admanzah I would kill her murderer,' I told him, ignoring his interruption.

He looked shaken for a second and then he burst out laughing. 'Tomorrow morning I drink coffee in Paris, in overlay. Go home, Detective Ishmael. To kill me, you destroy yourself. Americans too selfish for that. Just go home. You lost, no?'

'But I don't fight fair, Joshua,' I told him as I stood up to leave.

It was a long walk back and I used the time to try and figure out what to do next. Finally, as I neared home, it struck me: I hadn't lost yet, I had one last play.

❰ It was about four pm when I decided to drive into the KKK militia farm, aptly named Little Pentagon. This was Madison's dirty secret – we regularly stormed black neighbourhoods looking for drugs and guns, but we never touched the KKK militia, even though everyone knew that half the drugs and guns in the state were sitting right there on their farm.

To get to the farm, I had to drive through desolate looking neighbourhoods, where poor whites stared at me with a mixture of hate and envy. Poverty, here like elsewhere, whether in Allied Drive or Mathare, was the original sin.

Arriving at the farm gate, I showed my badge at the gate guarded by two rednecks with swastikas tattooed on their arms and AK-47s slung over their shoulders. The whole thing was a little overdone, they were outlandish caricatures of themselves, but that didn't make them any less dangerous.

My badge didn't faze the rednecks. What they wanted to know, though they didn't say it, was why a nigger cop was knocking on their door.

'I have some important business with your boss,' I said, opening the glove compartment and throwing in my badge, making sure that they could see my weapon was in there as well.

They called him on a walkie-talkie and then waved me through. I drove further into the farm. Nothing was grown here – in case it provided any kind of cover, I thought – and even the cabins had a temporary feel to them, like they were moved from time to time in order to confuse the enemy. Eventually, after getting myself lost a couple of times, I was directed to a cabin at the centre of the many others.

'What can I do you for?' James Wellstone asked when I opened the door. He was sitting in an armchair like some kind of a general, and looking at the maps of Dane County on the wall behind him. One would have thought he was in the middle of a major military operation.

'I have some information that might be of use,' I said, handing him a copy of the Never Again Foundation logbook.

He looked at it, whistling in surprise. 'Jews and niggers follow the dollar,' he muttered to himself. 'No offence, man, you okay by me,' he added, suddenly remembering I was there. 'Why are you giving me this?'

I explained the whole situation, how Joshua had not only escaped with the murder of a white girl, but was going back to Africa a richer man. 'Jim, I don't care about your fucked-up KKK war games,' I said to him pointing at the maps. 'But here is an opportunity for justice. Justice for your people.'

'And you, what do you get, Ishmael?' he asked.

'Justice ... '

'You are prepared to see a black man die for the murder of a white woman?'

I knew what he was driving at – I was a traitor to my race, no matter how I looked at it. But I had prepared for this. 'Genocide, justice for his role in the genocide. He killed a lot of my African brothers and sisters,' I said to him, knowing that the success of my mission depended on him believing me. 'Sometimes in history enemies find themselves on the same side. And it's not for one to judge the other ... they act because it's good for them. And afterwards they continue with their own battles. Let me ask you something, if black people had supported Hitler to defeat the British, Americans and communists wouldn't both your people and my people be better off? We would have Africa and you would have Europe. Now everything is a mess. And why? Because both sides were too consumed with hatred to seize an opportunity ... '

'I hate traitors, Detective, no matter the race. But you are right, today we are oppressed by the same governments,' Jim added.

It was then that I knew he would do it. He was striking a blow not just for his people, but showing cooperation was possible between two enemies for a larger goal. And more than that, he hated Joshua for being successful.

As Jim listened I explained how best to carry out the hit. Joshua was on a ten pm flight, so he would probably call a cab to pick him up at eight. All Jim had to do was steal a yellow cab. Joshua wouldn't be expecting any trouble, except from me, and looking outside his window and seeing the yellow cab would be enough. When he opened the door, Jim was to push him back inside and kill him.

'No fancy stuff, no photographs or souvenirs to show your little redneck friends, just walk out and drive off,' I said to him. I was being sarcastic, but he got my point.

'I will send someone to take care of this,' he said, but I knew it would be him. He wouldn't be able to pass up an opportunity like this. This was a chance for real action and it would turn him into a legend.

'It ends tonight,' I told him as I took the logbook from his desk.

He reached out and we shook hands.

I went to the station and left in a sleek black Mercedes-Benz 300 that we used for undercover surveillance. I drove to Maple Bluff and parked on the street two houses down from Joshua's place, blending in with other expensive cars. It was close to eight pm and I knew that Joshua would have already called a cab. I called the main offices, pretending to be him, and cancelled his request, saying that a friend had offered me a ride. The dispatcher called me an idiot but she did as I asked.

A few minutes later I saw Jim and one of the KKK goons drive by in a yellow cab. They pulled up a little way along the street and Jim got out and walked up the path to Joshua's house. As I had predicted, I saw Joshua peer through a window to verify it was the cab he had ordered. A few seconds later Joshua opened the door and Jim pushed him back into the house.

I drove the Mercedes past the cab. It looked like I was

simply looking for a place to turn around and the guy in the cab didn't make much of it. Why would he? I rolled down my window and slowed down when I came by him a second time. He was about to roll down his window when he recognised me and went for his gun. I shot him twice through his window.

Unscrewing the silencer I climbed out of the car and walked up the path to Joshua's house. I saw a flash and then a minute or so later Jim was closing the door behind him, tucking his gun into the small of his back. He saw me and stopped, trying to figure out what was going on. Then he started to smile nervously.

'Your gun, Jim, don't put it away,' I advised him as I raised mine.

He realised that if he went for his gun I was going to shoot him, so he raised his hands and went down on his knees on the porch. He might as well have taken his chances because I wasn't going to let him live. I shot him twice in the chest – the gunshots resounding loudly in the quiet neighbourhood. They would call the cops. I wanted them to.

I stepped over Jim's body and reached for the door handle, but as my hand met the cool metal I felt something tear into my shoulder, the force of it flinging me against the closed door. I whirled around to see Jim struggling to take aim again, but he was too weak to move fast enough. I shot him three times before he somehow managed to roll off the porch.

The bullet had lodged in my shoulder. I was just plain lucky, and in spite of the blood flowing furiously down my back I knew I would live. Opening the door, I staggered into the house. Joshua lay on the floor, still conscious but bleeding heavily. He had a bullet wound in his stomach, but most of the blood was from his femoral artery. Jim had wounded him, and then the bastard had cut his thigh open so that he could bleed to death. I couldn't have planned it better.

'You kill me ... you become monster,' he gasped. 'Call ambulance, I leave country ... never come back.'

'It's too late, Joshua,' I said to him, looking down at him as his life literally flew out of him.

'Then make me die,' he implored as he took a deep breath, trying to hold on to life.

I pulled up a stool, making sure his blood would not flow to where I was and sat down. 'Tell me, Joshua Hakizimana, how does it feel to know that in a few minutes you will be dead?' I asked him.

I finally understood O. Only what you do when you meet the Joshuas of this earth matters. Everything else – what you could have done, what some prosecutor or attorney says – is details.

Joshua tried to say something, but he was almost gone and I could see the panic in his eyes. He took a few deep breaths and tried to speak again but to no avail. Finally, he tried to write something with his blood, but there was too much on the floor and he only succeeded in swirling it around. He managed a small smile, half dangerous, half humorous, only his eyes had already lost their light. Then he lost consciousness and died.

As I stood up I almost slipped and fell. I looked down to find that the blood flowing from my shoulder had made a thin stream to Joshua's large pool of blood. I suppose that when I had thought that he was trying to write something he had in fact been mixing up our blood, trying to say that we had become one.

I walked outside. A small crowd was already forming. Someone had called in the shooting and I could hear sirens getting closer and closer. Soon the place was swarming with cops and I was surprised by how much I didn't feel like one of them. The Chief arrived and I explained what had happened: I had dropped in earlier in the day to see Joshua and he had told me that he was leaving the country. I had promised to give him a ride and was surprised to find a cab outside when I came to pick him up. Recognising the driver I had asked him to get out of the cab, but he had raised his weapon. I had had no choice. On the porch I had shot Jim as he was going for his gun. By the time I had made it to Joshua he was dead.

'Tell me something, Ishmael,' the Chief said in exasperation. 'Why did you need the Benz? You planned this whole thing didn't you?'

'Chief, I wanted to get him to the airport in style, him being a big shot and all,' I replied.

The Chief knew that I knew that it didn't matter what story I told. The KKK leader had killed Joshua, the vindicated hero, and I had shot him. Racial politics made it such that no one would ask questions. Rich white folk and rednecks do not get along. They never have. Over the years I had learned that Maple Bluff whites were as scared of white trash as they were of black gang-bangers. The death of Jim would be of no consequence, although the irony was that Jim had killed Joshua believing he was protecting a race that had long given up on his kind.

The Chief suddenly grabbed my arm and pulled me away from the rest of the men. 'Ishmael, can I ask you something?'

'Sure, Chief,' I said, slightly alarmed.

'How was it?'

'How was what, Chief?' I knew what he was asking, but I wasn't going to give it to him easy. I had nearly died over there.

'How was Africa? How was it for you?'

'Well, Chief, Africa is just Africa … just like the US is the US. I could have died there, but then again I could have died here. I found love there, I think. But I had it here, once,' I answered.

He looked at me and cleared his throat. 'Who cares about that shit, man. I mean, how was it for you in Africa?'

'Africa is the people, Chief,' I said, trying to answer him. 'But you gotta go see the people for yourself … sit down, talk, eat, fight and love with them.'

Then the adrenalin was gone and suddenly the pain was almost unbearable.

'Let the boys take you to hospital …' the Chief said with a chuckle, reaching out to hold me up before I lost consciousness. 'Take some time off, find a wife, do something.'

It was finally over and for the first time in a long time I felt content. It was as if I had left myself and gone somewhere and had only just returned.

❝ Two weeks or so later I was lying on the couch in my apartment when my cell rang. It was O. I was glad to hear from him – my shoulder had yet to heal and I had spent the last few days locked up in my apartment depressed as hell, the feeling of euphoria I had experienced that day outside Joshua's house had not lasted long. Two days earlier I had been to the grocery store, to stock up, and had left feeling disgusted. I had wanted to throw up – the chicken, so full of chemicals that it looked white, the giant oranges and bananas, all the fat motherfuckers and their motherfucking fat little bastards crying at the counter for candy that would rot their teeth. 'Africa is the people, so the US must be the people,' I found myself muttering over and over.

The following day was a Sunday and with nothing better to do I had pulled myself out of bed and made it to church. On my way there it had started raining. The mid-morning sun had been quite hot and when the rain had hit the pavements and tarred roads the air had suddenly been filled with dust and a light wetness. Then, for just a second, I had not been entirely sure where I was – back in Madison or in Eastleigh.

In the church, surrounded by folk I had known all my life, I had felt a warmth returning that had been lost to me since that night when I first stared down at Macy Jane Admanzah's body. But it was when the choir's guitarist had started to play the opening chords of *Amazing Grace* that I had finally felt something stir in my heart. He had played two verses solo, using a metal slide, and unlike Muddy's guitarist, who had run the slide across the frets so that the sound was rough, the choir's guitarist let the slide linger on a note – so that it hung in the air. And when the choir had finally joined in the sopranos had sung above the guitar, the tenors along with it and the bass underneath, each competing with each other and yet in harmony, the sound rising and rising until the whole church stood as one; some singing, some crying, some dancing. This was where I belonged, I realised as I looked around me. I needed to live my life in an intense place, a crucible. But then the service had ended and whatever had stirred – a feeling of belonging, of being embraced by voices whose register was an intense thirst for life – had died away.

'Look, man,' O said. 'I was just sitting here watching the old Ali-Foreman fight. Man, Ali was the business. Listen, I had a revelation. In life, you are either an Ali or a Foreman. People remember Ali as Ali. They remember Foreman as the funny old guy who fought Ali. You have to decide. Africa will make you Ali, America a Foreman …'

'What the fuck are you trying to say, O?' I asked, interrupting him.

'Private detectives … let us set up shop. We shall be the first international private eyes, you and I …'

I remained silent.

'Imagine all the assholes we can bring down …' he said, trying to convince me. 'For a hefty fee, of course.'

I started weighing up his offer as soon as he hung up. The truth of it was that in the US, if I tried hard enough, Mo and I would perhaps finally end up together and maybe make a good life for ourselves – kids, grandkids, et cetera. But I wanted more. I had seen some of the world and looked into an abyss so dark and cruel that I could never forget it. In Africa I could live out my contradictions, or at least my contradictions would be reconciled by the extremes of life there.

I looked at my little study full of files about dead people. I felt like I was in a stranger's apartment. Yes, I lived there – I recognised the wooden table, the clothes and photographs on the walls – but everything was from my past, there was nothing from the present. Perhaps I too had become something in need of solving. I had to move. It made sense. I could belong anywhere. I would choose Africa. There I had hated and loved like nowhere else.

There was Muddy and O. There was Janet. There were things to do there. I wasn't superfluous. I was useful and needed. What more could I have wished for? Why not see what happened?

I called the Chief, told him I was done and hung up on him before he tried talking me into staying. I wanted to live at one hundred degrees centigrade – all or nothing all of the time – and maybe do some good while at it.

Think me crazy, but I left the US at the height of my career for another beginning in that same Africa I had left.

MUKOMA WA NGUGI was born in Illinois but raised in Kenya. The son of world-renowned African writer and Nobel finalist, Ngugi wa Thiong'o, his own poetry and fiction has been short-listed for the Caine Prize for African writing in 2009, and for the 2010 Penguin Prize for African Writing. He lives in Stamford, Connecticut.

M MELVILLE INTERNATIONAL CRIME